Coalescence

A Holiday Collection

Coalescence

A Holiday Collection

By: Megan Mary Moore, Signe Damron,
Jordan King and Etta Grace

Illustrated by Phil Weasley

SIGNE:TURE PUBLISHING

"There is something at work in my soul, which I do not understand." - Mary Shelley

---

"Then the Grinch thought of something he hadn't before. What if Christmas, he thought, doesn't come from a store. What if Christmas, perhaps, means a little bit more." - Dr. Seuss

Table of Contents

Table of Contents

Mother's Day

There are good girls, and there are bad girls. Good girls listen to their grown-ups. They don't cry, and they love their mommy. My name is Penny. I'm five years old, and I'm a good girl. My baby sister, Sunny, was bad.

Sunny cried more than I knew anyone could. She cried more than she didn't. Last year, a girl in my class named Katie cried every morning when her daddy dropped her off at school. She cried loud and wet and sad. She'd hiccup during circle time, and her face would still be wet and snotty during snack time. But by the time we went outside to play, she wouldn't be sad anymore. She'd play and smile and giggle, and have forgotten she was upset at all.

Sunny never forgot she was upset.

And her cries were different. They didn't sound sad, they sounded angry, like she was mad at me. She never smiled, but Daddy said that was normal, that some little babies take longer to smile than others. But her face was red like an angry tomato, even when she wasn't crying.

Mommy and Daddy told me the baby wouldn't be able

to play right away, that she'd sleep a lot and she'd need lots of love and snuggles, and that it was my job to welcome her into the family. I knew she wouldn't be able to play games, but my friend Cyrus had a little baby at his house, a brother, and he was my favorite thing about playdates with Cyrus. Before I went to Cyrus's house, he told me that his baby couldn't talk or walk or play right, and that frustrated him. But his baby was so cute—he had tiny little fingers and toes and big eyes that watched you all the time. His mommy said he learned by watching with his big blue eyes. He had big, sweet cheeks that got bigger when he giggled, and he giggled a lot. Everything Cyrus and I did made him laugh. And he smelled good when you kissed his bald head, like baby powder and baby shampoo. I thought Sunny would be like that. I wanted Sunny to be like that.

But I didn't like to look at Sunny. Her eyes were beady and black, like bug eyes, and she always smelled rotten. Even after a bath and a diaper change, she still smelled like rotten food and poop.

I heard Sunny cry at the hospital when I met her, and it hurt my ears. But the sounds Sunny made in the middle of the night after she came home didn't just hurt my ears, it hurt my whole body. She sounded like scary sounds that some houses played on their porches for trick or treat. But this wasn't trick or treat, this was nighttime in my cozy, warm bed, where Mommy and Daddy always told me I was the safest.

The first night Sunny came home, I didn't sleep at all. I was scared, sleepy, and I wanted Mommy. So I got up and went into the hallway. I started to walk to Mommy and Daddy's room, but then realized the crying was coming from there since Sunny slept in their room in a little baby bed called a bassinet. I didn't want to get closer to the sound, so I walked in the other direction, toward Daddy's office.

I thought that maybe Daddy might be working still, and maybe he hadn't gone to bed yet. Sometimes, Daddy stayed up late working on his computer, even when he'd worked all day.

When I pushed open the door to Daddy's office, he wasn't

working, but he was in his office. He was on the ground, curled up in a little ball underneath a blanket. He had earmuffs on, even though it wasn't cold outside, and it definitely wasn't cold *inside*.

"Babies cry a lot, Pickle," he told me.

I nodded at him, and he led me back to my room, gave me a big hug and kiss, and tucked me back into bed while Sunny screamed with Mommy in their bedroom.

Daddy told me the same thing the next night when I came into his office when I couldn't sleep. And the night after that. "Babies cry a lot, Pickle." On the fourth night, he said the same words, but he sounded like a toy whose batteries were running out. His eyes only opened halfway, and the words dribbled out of his mouth like drool when he fell asleep on the couch on movie nights.

After that, he gave me a new sound machine shaped like a turtle. It lit up and played all kinds of sounds, like whales and rain and piano music. And you could make it loud, a lot louder than my old sound machine. So every night, I'd start it quiet, then click the arrow button to make it louder and louder until, finally, it wouldn't go any louder, and Sunny's screeches sounded like another noise in the rainforest, with the monkeys and toucans and the thunder.

I didn't love school until Sunny was born. I never cried when Mommy dropped me off like Katie did, but sometimes, I'd pretend to not feel good in the morning when Mommy came to wake me up. Even when I knew I wasn't really sick, I'd ask to stay home. But she always knew when I was just pretending, and she was good at reminding me about special things at school I didn't want to miss. Those things always ended up being fun, but I still wished I could snuggle with Mommy on the couch all day instead. It never seemed fair that we only stayed home and snuggled when I was really sick, too sick to stay awake for the movies or play games with Mommy. After Sunny was born, I couldn't wait to go to school every day. I'd wake up even earlier than Mommy and Daddy and get dressed and wait at the kitchen table for breakfast, wanting to be as far away from Sunny as possible.

I never napped at school until Sunny was born. It was boring, and I'm a big girl who doesn't need naps. And lying still was hard, especially when the sun would shine through the windows into my eyes even when I closed my eyelids.

When I fell asleep at school for the first time, I didn't remember it at all. I lay on my blue cot and pulled my unicorn blanket up to my chin, and when I opened my eyes, everyone in the class was playing again and I was the only one still lying down.

One day, I lay on my cot in the classroom, pulled my unicorn blanket up to my chin, and closed my eyes. But when I opened them, I was in the office, where the bad kids get sent to "cool down" and where Mommies and Daddies have meetings with the teachers.

I cried because I didn't know how I got there. I was still on my cot, still snuggled up, but I was in the wrong place. And I worried that I had done something really bad while I was asleep. "Penny, good morning," Mel, one of my teachers, whispered to me. But it wasn't morning, I knew it wasn't. "You seemed really sleepy today, and we thought you might need a little extra nap time where it was quiet. I hope that's OK." She kneeled next to my cot, and her smile felt as warm as my blanket. I nodded, but snot still ran from my nose, and I sniffed it up, hard.

"Do you need a hug, Penny?" Mel asked. I didn't say anything, but I sat up and slid from my cot onto her lap and rested my head on her chest, getting it wet and snotty. It made me think about how long it had been since I had cuddled with Mommy. Not since Sunny was born. She was too busy for cuddles and hugs now.

Me and Mel stayed like that for a long time before she told me that grown-ups would be here soon to pick up the children. That made me cry again. I didn't want to go home. I didn't even want to go to the car where Sunny would be strapped in the car seat next to me, screaming, angry, and stinky.

Mel held me and walked me out to Mommy's car while

I cried. All the other children saw me, and all of their parents. I was embarrassed because I wasn't a good girl anymore. I was turning into a bad girl, like Sunny. Sunny was changing me into a bad girl.

Mommy started not to look like my Mommy anymore. I thought maybe she looked different because she wasn't just *my* mommy anymore. My mommy was the most beautiful person ever, even though she told me a lot of times that it doesn't matter how you look. Her hair was black and silky smooth, even before she brushed it in the morning. Her skin was so soft, and she smelled like clean laundry, even when she had dirty clothes on.

Now that she was Sunny's mommy, she was almost as scary as Sunny. The skin under her eyes was purple and dark, and her lips were scaly. Her hair was different now, and the top of her head was turning gray and wasn't soft anymore. It was frizzy and crazy. She always smelled like milk, and it wasn't a bad smell, but it reminded me of Sunny.

Sunny drank her mommy's milk all day. It's the only time she wasn't crying. But that was when Mommy cried.

Mommy and Daddy told me about how the baby would drink the milk from Mommy's boobs and how important it was for Sunny to have Mommy time. They didn't tell me it would hurt Mommy. I asked Mommy if she had done that with me when I was little, and she said yes, it was one of her favorite parts of me being a baby. I tried to remember what that must have felt like, but I couldn't. And that made me sad.

I watched Mommy feed Sunny the day after they got home. They sat in the rocking chair next to Sunny's bassinet. Sunny was scream-crying again, but Mommy stayed calm and unbuttoned her shirt. Sunny found the nipple and put it in her mouth. And like magic, Sunny was quiet. But then Mommy said, "Ow!" really loud. Her body did a jump backward into the rocking chair, like she was trying to get away from Sunny. But Sunny jumped with her and reached her little baby hand up to Mommy's boob and grabbed it so hard that Mommy's skin turned white under Sunny's fingers. Mommy's eyes watered.

"Daddy! Daddy, come here! Sunny is hurting Mommy!" I screamed in a voice that I knew was too loud for inside, but I didn't care because Mommy was being hurt and it was an emergency. Daddy came running from his office, scared.

"Honey, honey, are you OK?" I didn't know if he was talking to me, Mommy, or Sunny.

"She bit me," Mommy said to Daddy, but she didn't stop looking at Sunny.

"She doesn't have teeth, honey." Daddy sighed and smiled, like he had gotten scared for no reason.

"But...she did. She bit me," Mommy said, staring at Sunny like she was scared she'd do it again. I was scared she'd do it again. And she did.

Mommy stopped saying "Ow!" when she fed Sunny, but she'd make a pain face the whole time. And Sunny would grab Mommy like she knew she wanted to get away. Mommy's face was always shiny and wet from tears when she fed Sunny, but neither of them made a sound. And Mommy fed her more and more once we found out it was the only time she would stop crying.

Daddy loved Sunny more than he loved Mommy and me. I know that because he changed all the rules for Sunny. Daddy said the TV was bad for babies, so we stopped watching it as soon as Sunny was born. We stopped family movie night, and I wasn't allowed to watch cartoons before school anymore like I used to. I was upset, but I didn't say anything because I wanted to be a good girl.

And Mommy wasn't allowed to eat or drink some things anymore. Before Sunny, we'd all eat breakfast together, and Mommy and Daddy would drink their coffee. After Sunny was born, Daddy and I ate breakfast while he would drink coffee and Mommy sat on the couch to feed Sunny.

There was one time during breakfast, when Daddy was in the bathroom, Mommy walked into the kitchen with Sunny still on her boob and picked up Daddy's coffee mug to sip it. But Daddy walked in as she did.

"Charlotte, you know you can't have that."

"Oh, come on, Chris. I'm running on no sleep here." She smiled at him, but her face was still sad, like she was frowning.

"Fine, if you think it's a good idea for our infant to drink coffee, be my guest."

Mommy put Daddy's coffee cup down and walked away. After that, Daddy and I went through a coffee shop drive-through every day before school so the coffee smell didn't "tempt" Mommy.

It made me sad to see Mommy not allowed to do things. I used to think that when you grew up and became a mommy, you were allowed to do whatever you wanted. I think it used to be that way before Sunny was born.

One night, I was in my room, awake from Sunny's screaming, when I heard another scream, not from Sunny and not from the rainforest animals on my sound machine. I sat up fast and ran to the door to listen. It was Daddy. I'd only heard Daddy yell once when I ran into the street last summer. I don't even remember why I did it; all I remember is Daddy's voice, loud and mean. He sounded even louder and meaner now, and I wasn't scared. I was relieved because, finally, Daddy was yelling at Sunny. Finally, he was mad at her. I reached for the doorknob and opened my door to listen. But he wasn't yelling at Sunny,

"She is an *infant*, Charlotte! And you are fucking insane." Mommy was crying, quieter than Sunny, but loud enough for me to hear.

"No, no, no, there is something wrong with that child…"

"The only thing wrong with Sunny is that she doesn't have a mother who loves her."

"I try! I try every single day to love that thing!"

"*Thing*? Charlotte, listen to yourself. She is our daughter."

"I'm trying, Chris!" Mommy cried.

"Try harder." Daddy didn't yell that exactly, but said it in a very serious voice. It scared me.

I think it was true that Mommy didn't love Sunny. But Sunny didn't love anyone.

After that night, I decided that I'd try too. The next day, I was coloring in the living room and Sunny was in her bouncy chair, a little baby chair set on the floor and propped so she could see everyone. She knew how to move her body to make herself rock back and forth and bounce. Her face was red and scrunched like it always was, and every few minutes, she'd scream. Not all the time, just as soon as you could forget about her last scream, she'd scream again.

Mommy was lying on the couch, falling asleep. Her blinks got slower and slower, until her eyes didn't open, and then Sunny would scream and Mommy's eyes would open again, wide and scared.

I decided to draw Sunny a picture. Even if she couldn't understand that the picture was for her, I had this idea that I'd draw it and show her, and then maybe she'd smile at me. And we would love each other, how sisters are supposed to.

I drew a picture of me and her and Mommy outside on a sunny day. I drew Sunny smiling in Mommy's arms, and I didn't draw her red, even though she was red in real life. In my picture, she looked like a whole new baby.

When I finished, I held it up to her to show her.

"This is for you, Sunny," I said. "Do you like it?" I knew she couldn't say anything back, but I thought it was nice to ask.

She made a funny face at the picture and a deep gurgling sound in her throat. Then she threw up. Only the throw up didn't go down her chin. It came straight out at me like a hose squirting water.

The picture I made got covered in yellowish-white throw up. Some got on my hand and my face and my lap. That was the last time I tried to love Sunny.

Mommy and Daddy used to talk about me all the time to everyone. Every time I heard them talking to other grown-ups, they were talking about me. At least, those were the times I paid attention. They said sweet, nice things that made me smile, especially when Sunny was still in Mommy's belly. People in the grocery store or the park would stop Mommy to talk to her.

They'd say, "Congratulations," which I learned was something that you were supposed to say when someone is about to have a baby. And Mommy would pat my head and say, "This one was so easy, we thought, why not have another?" or "We know that Penny will be the best big sister. She's such a good girl."

I never heard Mommy or Daddy talk about Sunny until one day, when Daddy was at the grocery store and Mommy spent a really long time in her room trying to make Sunny go to sleep for her nap. Sunny hated naps even more than sleeping at night, but that didn't stop Mommy from trying every day. Usually, Mommy would give up and let Sunny drink her milk, even when it wasn't time for her to eat. Mommy would sit on the couch with her pain face and stare at the TV, even though it was never on because of Daddy's rule.

That day, though, Mommy didn't let Sunny drink milk during naptime. Instead, she left Sunny in her bassinet and shut the bedroom door while Sunny screamed. Mommy came downstairs to the living room where I was doing my jungle puzzle, and Sunny was screaming louder than I'd ever heard her before. I know you're not supposed to do that, and I thought about how mad Daddy would be that Mommy wasn't snuggling Sunny like he always said we needed to. Mommy walked by me really fast with her phone in her hand and went into the downstairs bathroom, the one by the front door. She slammed the door hard, and it made me jump. Then I heard her voice.

"Mommy, I don't know what to do." Mommy's mom is Grandma. She was talking on the phone to Grandma, but I'd never heard her say, *Mommy* before. I always thought it was something that only little girls called their mom. Slowly, I walked over to the bathroom door. I was scared to see her so sad, but I wanted to hear what she was saying more, so I walked up to the door and pressed my ear against it.

"Something is wrong with that baby." Mommy *did* sound like a little girl—she was crying so hard she sounded like she was underwater, the same way I sounded in swim lessons when stuck my head under the water and said words, wet and bubbly.

"Penny was never like this. She was so sweet. She's always been such a good girl, even when she was a baby. But this baby, *this* baby… Her face… Her face is so red and angry, and her eyes are mean. I think, no, I *know* she is evil."

I didn't know what evil was, but Sunny did have a red angry face and mean, scrunchy eyes. Maybe that was what was wrong with her. She wasn't a normal baby, she was evil.

"We've been to the doctor. He said it's just colic, but it's not. It's something worse, I know it." Mommy's cries got quieter. "No, no, I don't want to go to the doctor. There is nothing wrong with me. There is something wrong with *her*."

The next day before school, when Daddy and I went through the drive-through at the coffee shop, he looked at me in the car mirror and said, "I'm gonna talk to you like a grown-up right now, Pickle." I nodded, looking back at him. His forehead seemed even wrinklier than usual.

"I know that having a new baby in the house is hard. Babies need a lot of attention. We told you that before Sunny was born." I didn't say anything.

"No, no, actually, that's not true." He shook his head fast, like he was thinking very hard. "Babies need *love*, Pickle, not just attention. They need to be loved." I nodded at him in the mirror, even though he wasn't looking at me. He was looking at the steering wheel, still shaking his head and thinking really hard. "Right now, Sunny is only getting that love from me. And she needs love from you and Mommy too."

"But you don't hold her," I said.

"What?" Daddy looked up at the car mirror again like I just woke him up.

"You said you're the only one who loves her, but you don't hold her. Isn't that how you love babies?" I asked.

I had never seen Daddy hold Sunny, not since she came home from the hospital. Every morning, I saw him bop her on the nose before we went to school, and he changed her diapers. He even counted the number of diapers he changed to be funny. This morning, he told me and Mommy he'd changed thirty-seven of Sunny's diapers. He was proud of that. But it was Mommy who held Sunny, rocked Sunny, fed Sunny.

His eyebrows and mouth screwed up in a frown. "There are a lot of ways to show love, Penny," he said shortly and angrily. "You know, I don't know if this store sells cake pops." He looked out the window, mad. I knew he was lying because two days ago we got pink cake pops here before school. I didn't know why Daddy was lying to me, but it made me mad. The car in front of us moved, so Daddy drove toward the window where we ordered.

"Sunny is evil." I said it to make him feel mad too. And after I said it, I knew I shouldn't have. Daddy looked in the mirror at me with mean black eyes that were just like Sunny's. He forgot to stop the car. We slammed into the car in front of us with a big bang.

"Fuck!" Daddy yelled. He got out of our car and talked to the person in the car in front of us for a long time. I didn't get a cake pop.

That day, Aunt Maggie picked me up from school. I love Aunt Maggie; she wears pink lipstick and red nail polish and perfume, and she lives in an apartment all by herself. But I wasn't excited to see her. I'd never ever been picked up from school by anyone who wasn't Mommy or Daddy, especially as a surprise. And I was nervous something was wrong.

"I missed you, my Lucky Penny!" Aunt Maggie said when I walked out of the gate. "So when your daddy called me and asked me if I wanted to spend some time with you, I said, *'Duh'*!" She smiled, and I giggled, feeling less nervous. "And guess what? I brought treats."

We walked over to the picnic table by the school playground, and Aunt Maggie pulled out a white paper box from her big bag. Inside the box were two pink cupcakes.

"Would you like to come stay with me for the week?" She licked the pink icing off her cupcake, and I did too.

"How long is the week, again?" I asked.

"Today is Monday, so you'll stay with me tonight,

Tuesday, Wednesday, Thursday, Friday, Saturday, and Sunday."

"Seven nights?" I asked, looking down at the seven fingers I was counting on. I slept over at Aunt Maggie's house before when Mommy and Daddy had a date night, but never for more than one night. Aunt Maggie nodded and took a bite of her cupcake. "And Mommy and Daddy are going to come get me after seven days?" I asked.

"Yes, ma'am." She smiled a big smile, and her teeth looked so white and pretty next to her pink lips.

Mommy and Daddy didn't pick me up after seven days. They picked me up after thirty days. At first, I was really sad sometimes, especially at bedtime, especially before Aunt Maggie bought the same turtle sound machine to help me sleep. After I got my turtle, though, I had fun at Aunt Maggie's apartment. She didn't have any toys, and the only things in her refrigerator were wine, nail polish, and ketchup, but she had so many movies to watch on her TV. And she never made me turn it off. The TV stayed on all day long. It never turned off, only the volume got turned down when it was time to sleep and I turned my turtle on. I slept in front of the TV in Aunt Maggie's living room on a couch that could turn into a bed. She called it a futon, but I kept forgetting that word and saying crouton. Aunt Maggie thought that was really funny.

Snow White was my favorite movie to watch at Aunt Maggie's. I put it on the TV every night that I stayed with her. Even when things were really sad and scary for Snow White, she stayed sweet and kind and kept being a good girl. And because she was such a good girl, she got a happy princess ending. I could do that. I could be a good girl when things were sad and scary, and then I'd get a happy princess ending.

My least favorite was the movie about the ice queen and her sister. The ice queen was so mean to her sister, even after their mommy and daddy died. That's how Sunny would be to me, I knew it. In the movie, though, they make up and become friends at the end. That seemed more pretend than all the ice magic.

Really, Mommy and Daddy didn't pick me up at all. One day, after we ate chicken nuggets and french fries for dinner, Aunt Maggie packed up the car and drove me home.

That's when I asked Aunt Maggie why I stayed so much longer than seven days.

"Sometimes, Mommies and Daddies like to spend a little extra time alone with their new baby," she explained.

"Without me?"

"I think that your parents are having a hard time adjusting to having a new baby in the house. It has nothing to do with you." But I didn't believe that.

"You wait in the car, Lucky Penny," she told me when we pulled into the driveway behind Daddy's car. "I just have to go inside and talk a little to Chris and Charlotte first, OK?" She looked at me in the rearview mirror and winked.

Aunt Maggie got out of the car, walked up to the door, and rang the doorbell. She turned around and looked at the car while she waited at the door. She waved, and I waved back. Neither of us smiled.

When Daddy opened the door, he didn't look happy to see Aunt Maggie. He stepped outside and looked behind her to see her car parked behind his. When he saw me, he smiled really big, like a pretend smile, and waved. I didn't wave back. He looked at Aunt Maggie, and his smile disappeared. He frowned, and I saw his wrinkles all the way from where I was sitting. Aunt Maggie threw her arms in the air, and Daddy pointed his finger really close to her face, almost touching her. She turned around fast and stomped back to the car, angry.

Even though I didn't hear what they said, I knew Daddy didn't think that it was time for me to come home and Aunt Maggie did.

"OK, Penny, I had so much fun with you! Give Mommy and Baby Sunny a big hug for me, OK?" Aunt Maggie said as she unbuckled me from my car seat. I climbed out, and she unloaded her trunk of all my things: my overnight bag, my backpack, my lunch box, my pink pillow. She put them all in a big pile and set my turtle sound machine on top.

Aunt Maggie kissed the top of my head, got in her car, and drove away and left me standing alone in the driveway next to my pile of stuff. I was too afraid to go inside. I really didn't want Daddy to point his finger in my face like he had with Aunt Maggie. He didn't want me to come home anyway, that's why he didn't pick me up after seven days. That's why he fought with Aunt Maggie. It wasn't about spending special alone time with Sunny; he was mad I'd said Sunny was evil, so he'd sent me away. He thought I was a bad girl. I cried a little until I remembered that good girls don't cry, and I wiped my tears with my dress.

I didn't have a good sleep that night because I missed the light from the TV at Aunt Maggie's apartment, and could still hear Sunny screaming, even when I turned on both of my turtle sound machines. The thought of walking out of my room to find Daddy in his office and asking him to tuck me back in crossed my mind, but then I remembered his fight with Aunt Maggie. I needed to prove to him that I was a good girl now and I deserved to come home, so I turned on my light and played with my baby dolls instead.

I used to play with my baby dolls all the time, especially when Sunny was still in Mommy's belly because I was so excited to have a baby sister. But after Sunny was born, I didn't even want to look at my baby dolls anymore. Babies weren't fun anymore.

That night, I looked really hard at my favorite baby doll. She was so much cuter than Sunny, with big bright eyes and a happy face and cuddly body. At first, I held her to my body the way Mommy did with Sunny when she was feeding her. Then I burped the baby doll and bounced her and rocked her and snuggled her. I laid her down in my bed, all cozy and sweet, but then I got mad. Really, really mad.

Sunny was a bad baby, a bad girl. She stole my mommy and hurt her all the time, and she was making Daddy hate me. She was the bad one who needed to go live with Aunt Maggie, not me. And then I hit the baby doll. Over and over and over and over again. I picked it up and slammed its head on my headboard until its head was all dented and smushed.

I must have fallen asleep then because Daddy's and Mommy's voices woke me up the next morning from the hallway. Sunny wasn't crying, so I knew she was drinking milk from Mommy.

"Charlotte, you know I do this every year," Daddy said. If Mommy said anything back, I couldn't hear it. I climbed out of bed and opened my door, expecting to see Daddy smile and say, "Good morning, Pickle!" But he didn't. Because I wasn't a good girl anymore. He didn't even look at me. He kept looking at Mommy, who was sitting in her room in the rocking chair next to their bed, feeding Sunny. Daddy had his work clothes on and a tie, but I knew that it was Sunday and that he never went to work on Sundays. But he was in the hallway like he was about to go downstairs and leave.

"Look, you know how my mom is. She'll make my life hell if I don't spend Mother's Day with her."

I didn't know what hell meant, but I knew it was a bad word. And I never heard Daddy say bad words around Sunny. He was always really careful about what he said around her because babies should only hear nice, love words, not mean ones.

Mommy looked like a scary ghost from a movie. Her face was really white, and the circles under her eyes looked almost black instead of purple. She looked at Daddy for a long time. And then she screamed, "*I* am a mother!" Spit flew out of her mouth. I saw almost all of her teeth. They were yellow and looked ready to bite, like an angry dog. I put my hands over my ears as fast as I could because I knew Sunny would start crying. But she didn't. She stayed still and quiet on Mommy's boob.

Daddy stepped backward as if someone had pushed him. I felt tears in my eyes, and I blinked really hard to make them stop before they came out. But I couldn't stop the pee that came out and soaked my panties and pj pants.

"Leave." The voice came from Mommy, but it wasn't her voice. She sounded like an old lady with a sore throat trying to talk. "Get the fuck out." Her teeth were still showing, and she made a noise like a low, deep growl at Daddy. Daddy left without saying goodbye to us.

After I went back into my room, I took my pee clothes off. I heard Daddy say it was Mother's Day. I remembered Mother's Day last year. Mommy and I went out to a special tea party restaurant. We ate cookies and cakes for lunch and drank tea, and I wore my most beautiful dress. It was white with pink flowers and had scratchy fabric under the skirt part that made it really poofy and pretty. I still had it in my closet.

I put on the dress. It was shorter than I remembered, and I couldn't reach the zipper in the back to zip it up. But when I looked in the mirror, I couldn't see that it wasn't closed in the back. The front still looked pretty.

I walked into Mommy and Daddy's room, excited to see what Mommy would say when she saw me. Maybe she'd tell me how pretty I looked, and she'd pick me up and twirl me around. But Mommy and Sunny were still in the rocking chair together, both of their eyes closed. They were both asleep.

I went downstairs to the kitchen. Since I was hungry, I opened the pantry and saw granola bars on a shelf. I dragged my step stool from the kitchen sink to the shelf and grabbed the box.

I went into the living room and turned on the TV because Daddy wasn't here and Sunny was upstairs. So I thought it was OK. I had learned how to work the remote at Aunt Maggie's house, so I found the princess movies fast. I watched *Snow White* and ate three granola bars. My mouth moved along with the words since I'd learned all of them, and sometimes, little bits of granola fell out of my mouth onto my dress. I brushed them off every time that happened, though, just in case Mommy came downstairs. I wanted her to see how clean and pretty I was in the dress.

She didn't come down until the movie was over, after Sunny started crying.

When I heard her footsteps on the stairs, I jumped up, turned off the TV, and threw away my granola bar wrappers so she'd see that I hadn't made a mess. When she came into the living room, she crouched down on her knees so her eyes were looking straight at mine.

"Penny, listen. Something is very wrong with Sunny," Mommy said.

"She's evil," I said. Mommy's eyes got wide, and she smiled wide with the same yellow dog teeth that she'd growled at Daddy with.

"Yes, yes, Penny! You know. You understand." Mommy reached out and tucked my hair behind my ears. Her hands were shaking.

My whole body shivered like it did when I took a big bite of a hot fudge sundae, and I felt a rush of hot and cold and sweet all over. Mommy knew I was a good girl again. I was Mommy's good girl again.

"I know how to save Sunny."

"You know how to make her not evil?" I asked. Sunny could be cute and sweet, like my baby doll. Mommy could fix her.

"Yes. I've known how to for a while, but Daddy doesn't understand like we do. So I had to wait until he wasn't here."

"Daddy doesn't love us anymore," I said to her.

"Daddy is a cocksucker," Mommy said, her dog teeth still closed. I didn't know what a cocksucker was, but I knew she was right. "I am a mother"—she said—"and I know what is best for my babies."

I am a good girl—I thought—*and my mommy needs my help.*

"What do we need to do?"

"A baptism."

Mommy explained to me that we needed to use water to clean the evil out of Sunny. But we needed to make sure that her whole body was clean, inside and out, and she wouldn't be happy about it. But we had to stay strong, even when she was really angry and screaming. The angrier she got, the better, because that was the evil leaving her body.

I was so busy being angry with Sunny that I didn't know

how badly I wanted Sunny to be good. But now that I knew she could be, I wanted it more than anything in the world.

Mommy filled up the bathtub with water, and I tried to imagine how we could be a happy family: Mommy, Daddy, me, and Sunny. Maybe when Sunny wasn't evil anymore, Mommy would have more time for me again, and she wouldn't be so tired. We could all go to a tea party together next year.

It was hard to imagine all of that, though, with Sunny screaming next to me in her bouncy chair on the bathroom floor.

When the bathtub was filled up higher than I'd ever seen it, Mommy unzipped Sunny's onesie while she wiggled and threw her arms and legs everywhere. Then Mommy held her up, naked, like they did with the baby lion in the movie with the talking lions. Sunny squirmed like a red, floppy fish in Mommy's hands. Mommy looked like she wanted to say something. I tried to figure out how she felt by looking at her face, but I couldn't. And then Mommy put Sunny under the water.

It happened like Mommy said it would. The evil left Sunny's body, and she screamed and wiggled really, really hard. She opened her mouth to scream under the water, and big bubbles rose up from her mouth. Mommy leaned over the tub and held her down with both of her hands. I didn't know a baby could be so strong. Mommy was trying really hard to keep her underwater. The tub overflowed, and water splashed everywhere.

"Penny, help me," Mommy said. "Get in the tub and help me." I did.

And then, Sunny was peaceful and quiet and finally looked like the sweet little baby sister I always wanted. I thought about the movie about the ice queen and her sister and how they hugged at the end, and I thought about hugging her then, even though she was slippery and wet. But I was still scared that she'd open her eyes and scream or throw up in my face like she had when I showed her the picture I made for her.

For a second, I wondered if Sunny wasn't evil anymore, if maybe Mommy would change back to the way she looked before Sunny was born. Maybe she'd transform like Cinderella before the ball, and sparkles would fall all over her while her hair turned soft again and her skin turned back to normal. Maybe her eyes would be bright and pretty again.

That didn't happen. She was soaking wet, just like me, just like Sunny. She looked even less like Mommy than she ever had before. Not mad, or sad, or happy. She stared at Sunny for a long time. Then she looked at me.

"Penny, it's your turn."

Mrs. Claus

I hate Christmas, and I hate working in an office. But I love office Christmas parties.

It's the one time a year when I can be myself around my boring ass coworkers; after a full year of turtleneck sweaters and biting my tongue to keep on the payroll, I finally get to be drunk and slutty with no consequence.

After a long night of drinking incredibly too much alcohol—and learning incredibly too much about my coworkers—the party is over. I'm the last one to leave the office, the one expected to lock up—not because I'm the most trustworthy, but because everyone else is already home and in bed with their husbands, wives, and little ones, hallucinating about dancing sugar plums.

I lock the office door behind me at 1:45 a.m., grateful I'm too drunk to be depressed about being at the office on a Friday night.

From the time I was expected to do chores at home, I've hated working. I have a vivid memory of locking myself in the bathroom for three hours after dinner one evening to avoid doing the dishes. I got out of the dishes that night, but my mother still brings it up as an example of how lazy I am at least once a year.

I've always hated work, but I hate the idea of domestic responsibilities even more.

My mom was a stay-at-home mom, and it was no secret that she resented it, that she resented us—me, my dad, and my brothers.

"Your dad started banging his secretary and left me with three snot-nosed brats" was the only information she shared when I asked about my father. She never became less bitter, and I never got any better. At twenty-three, I'm still a snot-nosed brat who hates doing as she's told, at least, according to my mother.

Almost all childhood memories of my mother include her refrain of "I hate my life," followed by, "One day you'll wake up and I'll be long gone." No matter how many times she threatened to abandon us, though, every morning she was still there, still exhausted, and still complaining.

The first dozen or so times I was relieved that she hadn't packed up and left in the middle of the night—the idea of being left alone and lost without my mother to cook or clean for me terrified me. I would sit awake at night and listen for the shut of the front door or the rolling wheels of her suitcase on the linoleum. I went through the pain of expecting her to leave for no reason, over and over, and as I got older, I got mad that she never made good on her promises to disappear.

"If you want to leave so bad, leave," I told her one morning as she frowned over her coffee.

"I would if I could, Clare. But I'm responsible for you brats."

That's when I realized I hated my mother, not just because she hated me, but because she hated herself so much, she could never allow herself to be happy. I vowed to myself then and there to never become responsible for anything or anyone.

I saw how miserable she was, how miserable *I* made her. That would never happen to me. I wouldn't be the disgruntled mom who hates her life and gets left alone to clean up the man's mess. I'd be the secretary who helps make the mess.

And now I am. After high school, I got my associate's degree in office administration and began working as a receptionist for an insurance company. And I only sleep with married men—attractive married men. Not as a kink, but to ensure I get the fun parts of a relationship while shirking any wifely responsibilities.

I turn away from the office door, and a blustery wind strikes my cheek like a slap. "I fucking hate the cold," I grumble to myself, pulling a cigarette out of an almost empty pack.

"You wouldn't do well where I'm from," says a deep smiling voice from behind me. Turning around, I see the Santa impersonator my boss hired for the night. I inspect him under the yellow shine of the streetlight. I hadn't interacted with him during the party, except to get a picture on his lap with Mina, the HR rep. We both sat on one of his knees and kissed his scratchy cheeks. He still has my bright red lipstick kiss on the side of his face. I could tell then that the beard was real, but now, seeing him without distractions, he does really look like the Santa Claus I used to imagine as a little girl, not that I believed in Santa for long.

My mom couldn't stand the fat man getting credit for the presents she bought and wrapped for my brothers and me every year. When I was five, on Christmas morning, before we got the chance to unwrap anything, my mother announced there was no Santa. That it was only a story parents told their kids to get them to behave, but we didn't behave anyway, so screw it. She was getting the credit from then on out.

"Oh shit, where are you from?" I ask the Santa impersonator through closed lips as I light my cigarette.

"Why, the North Pole, of course." He smiles at me, followed by a big belly laugh. "You don't plan on driving home in this condition, do you, young girl?"

"Welcome to Ohio. Everyone drives drunk. It might be more dangerous to drive sober."

"Good boys and girls don't drink and drive." He takes a step closer to me.

"Ah, I'm not a good girl, but if you were the real Santa, you'd already know that." I wink.

"I do. You've been on the naughty list every year since you were born, Clare." Santa smiles at me and strokes his beard. I cock my head at him. I don't remember telling him my name, but I've been shitfaced since 9 p.m., and it's possible I told him during the party while blacked out.

"Well, don't worry about me, Santa. I called a ride service. I'm just waiting for the car."

"Then it won't hurt you to have one last drink." He reaches inside his red and white fluffy jacket and retrieves a metal flask from an inside pocket. I take it from his hand as soon as he pulls it out, prompting him to bellow a cartoonish "Ho, ho, ho." Whatever is in the flask burns my throat, but doesn't touch my tongue long enough for me to get a taste.

"You have kids?" I ask, handing the flask back to him.

"Oh, ho, ho. I have kids. Over a billion."

"Ah, of course. That sounds like a nightmare." I drop my cigarette to the ground and grind it out with the sole of my red stiletto.

"You'll change your mind about that," he says.

Before I can get offended, I feel woozy.

"I don't feel so good." My knees grow weak, like I've gotten too heavy to hold myself up. I stumble backward in my heels and topple into Santa's arms.

Looking up, I see the Santa impersonator's wide, bearded smile. I fight to keep my eyelids open, but I can't.

When I wake, I peel my cheek from my shoulder, sticky with drool. I move to wipe the spit from my face and realize I've been tied up with sparkling silver tinsel that itches and digs into my bare arms, wrists, and ankles.

In front of me is a wooden table, and the Santa impersonator sits on the other side, hands folded, as if he was patiently waiting for me to come to.

To be honest, I expected to get kidnapped or raped at some point in my life. I'm aware that I'm drunk, scantily clad, and alone often enough to attract attention from the worst kind of men. I never thought that Santa Claus would be the one to do it, though.

"What do you want from me?" The words croak out of my dry mouth.

"I need a wife," he says, pouring two glasses of milk from a large glass pitcher on the table.

My mind races—a wife. I can work with that. I *am* going to get out of this. If there was one thing I know about men, it's how to give them what they want.

"I can help you with that, Mr. Claus," I say, pouting my bottom lip and looking up through my smudged lashes.

"Stop that! Stop whatever this is right now." He looks at me like I'm a naughty child acting out.

"You *do* need a wife to take care of you, don't you, big boy?" I shimmy in the chair, utilizing the slight range of motion the tinsel allows for.

"Stop it!" he yells, and slams the pitcher of milk on the table. "I need a wife to make my meals, clean house, and help me with the children." I stop shimmying, realizing my fate might be far worse than I first imagined.

"My wife recently passed, may she rest in peace, and I can't live without a woman."

"How did she die?" I scour my surroundings, looking for weapons or torture devices he may plan to use on me. But I see nothing out of the ordinary, other than a brightly lit Christmas tree in the corner.

"Reindeer accident. It's a pity. She was a good woman."

"Ah, there you have it, Santa. *I* am not a good woman. You said it yourself: I'm always on the naughty list."

"She was a lot like you when I brought her here too. I like a challenge." He smiles warmly and sips from his glass. "All of my wives come from the top of the naughty list. I tend to think of it as a kind of reform for you and good deed on my part. Look at it this way, you spent twenty-three years on the naughty list. Now you'll spend twenty-three as my missus, baking cookies, checking in on children, cleaning the suit." He pulls an imaginary speck of dust from his shoulder. "Not a bad deal, if you ask me."

"OK, can we drop the Santa thing just for a second and talk about what's going on here? I'm down to role play for the night or whatever, and hell, if we have fun, we can do it again sometime." I try to smile but cringe when I hear the obvious desperation in my voice. My fear is showing.

"Drop the Santa thing?" the man in the red suit across from me smirks.

"What's your real name?"

"Clare, since you were six years old, every year, you have asked me for the same thing."

It was true. Even though I knew Santa wasn't real, it didn't stop me from writing Christmas lists the same way other children prayed. What I wanted was too dark to tell God, let alone ask Him to make it happen. So, I asked what I considered another imaginary father figure, Santa Claus.

"I get requests like yours every year, but you, Clare, were persistent. Every year, the same thing. And every year, you made the naughty list. But you're not a little girl anymore. You're going to be my wife, and this year, you get exactly what you've always wanted."

The shrill ring of my cell phone cuts through the tension between us.

"Oh." Santa leans down and retrieves my purse from under the table. "We'll want to answer that." He reaches in and grabs my ringing phone. Adjusting his round glasses, he stares down his rosy nose at the phone. He slides the button to answer the call and presses the speaker button with his stubby finger.

"Clare, are you there?" It's my brother, Matt.

"Matt? Matt, please, I need help. I've been kidnapped. Please, help me," I say frantically. But Santa's stubby finger is quick to press mute.

"Clare, listen. Mom is dead." My heart drops into my stomach, and my eyes raise to meet Santa. He is calm and unsurprised. "It was awful. The Christmas tree…it caught on fire. *She* caught on fire. She…she really suffered, Clare." Matt's voice quivers, but he doesn't break into tears. Santa ends the call.

"You're welcome." Santa Claus winks at me. "OK"—he pats his knees and sighs—"we have a busy week ahead of us, dear, so I am off to bed." He stands, even taller and wider than I remember in the office parking lot.

I stare up at him in awe. The only words I can find are the ones I know to be true. "You're him."

He chuckles, a jolly, animated, "Ho, ho, ho."

Hadley-Bear

"This is a good opportunity for you to really get the experience of being a mom," Shelly says sweetly. I nod and smile just as sweetly in return, aware that I've never talked to her about wanting to be a mom.

I don't blame her for assuming I want children. She was my age when she married her husband, John, and just one year older than me when she gave birth to Hadley. I love kids, and as of this month, I'm a college graduate with no job prospects other than my usual summer babysitting job. So, yeah, it has occurred to me that *wife* and *mom* might be the most logical next steps for me. But every time I've thought about it, it feels wrong, like there's no way I could possibly be old enough to have a child. *I'm* still a child.

"You've been Hadley's sitter for what? Almost six years now?"

I nod again, trying not to look as bored as I feel.

This is the first time Shelly and John have been on a trip together without their ten-year-old daughter, which is why they're paying me good money to watch her for a week while they get drunk in Destin, Florida, free from the parental responsibilities they've been burdened with for practically their entire marriage.

"Wow, six years. This will be different, though. You know, with waking her up, walking to and from school with her. I know she seems pretty self-sufficient, but you'd be surprised how much she really needs us." Shelly's brow wrinkles as if she's realizing this for the first time.

I understand they're nervous about leaving her for so long, but I *have* been Hadley's sitter since I was eighteen and she was only four years old. Having spent every summer for the last three years with Hadley, I know everything I need to know to spend a week with her. That doesn't include every date night and family emergency they've needed a sitter for. I know her nighttime routine, what she likes to eat, ways to trick her into doing her homework, and I know just how good of a kid she is. I've had the luxury of being lenient because she's never pushed too far. An extra hour with her friends or an extra cookie or two after dinner is the most she's ever asked me for.

She sighs. "But we trust you, Heather. We know you won't let Hadley down."

"Tomorrow is the last day of school before summer— we're just going to be playing games and watching movies all day," Hadley says that night when I tell her it's time to turn off her iPad and go to sleep. Previously, I've only had to put her to bed on Friday or Saturday nights, when there was no consequence if she didn't go to sleep exactly at 9 p.m. But tonight is Thursday. She has school tomorrow morning, and I've already allowed her an extra twenty minutes of screen time.

"That means this is the last time that you have to go to bed early for three months," I say, hand outstretched expectantly, waiting for her to hand me the iPad.

"*Heather*," she whines in a voice that immediately

reminds me of how young she really is.

I hold my ground and wait for her to hand over her tablet. She does so before pulling her bright pink duvet over her head in a huff.

"Goodnight, Hadley-Bear," I say, and kiss her head through the duvet, getting a whiff of her strawberry shampoo, the same one she's used for as long as I can remember. I flip the light switch off and shut the door to her room.

John and Shelly would be pleased with how I handled that situation, I know. But I'm not. I've never wanted to be strict with Hadley, and I rarely have to. I hate seeing her pout, especially when that pout is directed toward *me*, the cool babysitter.

Honestly, I would have let Hadley stay up later tonight if I wasn't so eager to get back to the guest room and text my boyfriend, Brock. She's right, tomorrow is the last day of school, and of all the nights to stay up, tonight would be the one. And we had such a fun evening together. We made pizza, watched a movie while eating popcorn and gummy bears, and gossiped about all the kids at school. And finally, Hadley got screen time with her iPad in bed while I cleaned up. I feel bad that I had to end the evening for her, but now it's *my* screen time.

"Hey," I text to Brock the moment I close the door of the guest bedroom behind me.

"Everyone in bed?"

"Yes :)"

"Show me." I quickly strip off my shirt and jeans and take a hasty selfie of myself in my bra and panties, lying on the bed.

"Can I come over?"

I bite my lip, contemplating just how much trouble I'd be setting myself up for if I let him. If Shelly and John found out—which is all too possible considering how loud Brock's voice and footsteps are and how Hadley can't keep a secret to save her life—I would never be invited back to babysit. I'm not willing to risk that. Shelly and John pay well, and I can always use the money, not to mention I love Hadley. As badly as I want to see

Brock, the idea of not being able to see Hadley upsets me too much to risk it.

"I'm sorry :(Hadley is at school from 8:30-3 tomorrow though, come over?"

"I'm cutting grass tomorrow until 5"

A few seconds later.

"Let me come over tonight, I'll be quiet I promise."

I'd be lying if I said I wasn't tempted. The worst thing about coming home from college is being away from Brock. We live about thirty minutes from each other, which is a big deal considering, on campus, we rarely spent a night apart. I've only been home from school for two days, and every free second has been dedicated to thinking about Brock—his body, his hands… his hands on my body. And there is admittedly something sexy about fooling around with him while I'm supposed to be babysitting.

"I'm sorry, baby, I can't."

He leaves me on *read* for five minutes until he finally replies with, "Send me a video to hold me over?"

I hop out of bed and prop my phone against a framed photo of Hadley from a few years ago. She's standing in a sunflower field, and the sunflowers tower over her, her toothy grin demanding a gaze even among the big bright yellow flowers. I scoot the phone so it's completely covering the photo and record.

I've just unhooked my bra and slid the straps down my shoulders, prepared to shimmy it down my arms the way Brock likes, when I hear the tinny sound of voices from a television. For a second, I stare toward the door before pressing the record button to stop the video. I quickly put my bra back on, followed by the rest of my clothes as I piece together what could be making the noise. I've taken Hadley's iPad, and she doesn't have a television in her room…

I open the door to Shelly and John's dark bedroom and see Hadley on their king-sized bed, bathed in the eerie glow from the TV as she stares up at the huge screen mounted to the wall.

"Hadley, I said lights-out," I hear myself say in a voice I know all too well. It's not my voice, it's my mother's. My frustration with my voice is eclipsed by my frustration with Hadley. In all the years I've watched her, she's never pushed my limits like this. "Hadley!" I say again, louder, but she still doesn't look away from the television. I glance toward the screen to see what she's watching.

It's a wooden puppet show. Two carefully carved marionettes move jerkily in front of the camera. A British man's voice is speaking for them in a squeaky falsetto. "Jack, have you ever made toast in the bath before?" He answers himself in a similar squeak. "No, Will, the toast would get soggy!"

The two little boy puppets trot to a porcelain bathtub filled with water in the corner of the shot. On the floor next to it is a puppet-sized metal toaster.

"Hadley!" I yell this time, still fixated on the screen. In the corner of the screen, in bold letters, are the words Lunatic Looey's Puppet Show.

"Just let me finish it, Heather." Hadley's tone brings my full attention back to her. Gone is the little girl whine I heard just twenty minutes earlier. This is the defiance of a preteen.

"I said lights-out. That means all lights." I step in front of her view of the screen to grab her attention.

"But everyone is going to be talking about it at school tomorrow," she says, scooting a few inches to see around me. I hear the shrill shrieks of the puppeteer behind me, and I assume that one or both of the puppets have plunged into the bath with the toaster.

Hadley's eyes grow wide, and a smile crawls onto her face. I whip my body around and press the power button on the side of the television, glimpsing the marionettes convulsing violently in the tub, water splashing, wooden limbs wildly hitting the side of the tiny tub and each other, before the image turns to black.

"No!" Hadley shrieks, practically matching the pitch of

the puppets. "I want to see what happens!"

"They die," I say. "Now go to bed."

"They always die. The fun part is watching them die." I search her face for some proof that she's trying to get a rise out of me, but I'm only met with a cold, stubborn stare.

"Whatever that was, you shouldn't be watching it."

"It's literally for kids, Heather," she says, finally getting up, her skinny shoulder knocking into my arm as she passes me. "You don't get it." I follow her into her bedroom and watch as she climbs into bed. Even though she's doing what I've asked, her attitude makes me feel as if she's somehow won this argument.

"Goodnight, Hadley-Bear," I say again, from the doorway.

"Don't call me that," she says as I close the door.

In the time it took me to convince Hadley to go back to bed, Brock has sent me four text messages:

"Hello? Heather?"

"No video?"

"K I'm going to bed I have to be up at like 6."

"Night."

I take my phone and throw it on the bed, where it bounces and lands on the floor with a thud. Curling up on the bed, I stare at the wall, knowing I've pissed off both Hadley and Brock. I can't help but be annoyed with both of them; I couldn't give them exactly what they wanted when they wanted it, and they're making me feel shitty about it. That annoyance is clouded by a sense of sadness and loneliness. I can't handle their being mad at me, no matter how stupid the reason. I promise myself to make things right with both of them in the morning.

"You don't have to walk me," Hadley tells me on the front porch the next morning as we prepare to leave for school. She looks more mature today, as if our argument has somehow aged her. Her long chestnut hair is getting the golden highlights that only come out in summer, and she's wearing a daisy print tank top and denim shorts. Her hands are on her hips, and at this moment, I am desperate to make her like me again.

I have to walk her, and she knows that. But instead of arguing, I say, "I want to walk with you. I want to see your school." She rolls her eyes, and for the entire two blocks, walks several strides ahead of me so it looks as if we're two strangers.

As soon as she walks into the school doors without so much as a wave goodbye, I pull my phone out of my pocket and text Brock, though I know he's already at work for his dad's lawn care service and I don't know when he'll see it.

"I'm so sorry about last night, baby. I'll make it up to you, I promise ;)"

Six hours later, I wait outside of Hadley's school. Tomorrow is Memorial Day, the unofficial first day of summer, and the air is practically buzzing with the energy that only exists on the last day of school before summer break. There's a sense of eagerness and excitement, as well as the bittersweet knowledge that you'll never be right here in *this* class with *these* friends ever again. I find myself missing it, jealous of the children yelling and running across the schoolyard with a glee I worry I may never feel again.

Hadley appears with a blond girl, walking so close together that they could pass as one two-headed tween. They skip up to me, and I recognize the other girl as Rachel, one of Hadley's friends.

"Hi, Heather," Rachel says sweetly through a chapped smile. The pair of girls smell like sweat and dirt, like they've been playing outside all day. They probably have. I feel a twinge of sadness knowing I've stayed inside scrolling on my phone the entire time, hoping to hear from Brock, though I never did.

"Hadley wants to know if she can stay at my house tonight," Rachel asks me.

I've known Rachel almost as long as I've known Hadley. She's been in every sport that Hadley decided to try and eventually quit. And at every afternoon park trip, Rachel is there, begging Hadley to stay later than we'd planned to. I've met Rachel's mom several times too, though we've never talked about more than the weather or how big the girls are getting. I'm a babysitter and she's a mom, and we both understand playground politics well enough to know that she doesn't owe me more than a polite hello. Hadley has stayed over at Rachel's house a handful of times before, and Shelly and John trust Rachel's family.

"Please, Heather," Hadley asks, grabbing my hand. "I'm sorry for being bratty earlier." Her brown eyes meet mine, and I choose to believe that she's genuinely sorry, though part of me knows she's only apologizing so she can stay the night at Rachel's.

A million thoughts rush through my head, but only one thought sticks long enough for me to fully understand. Hadley won't be mad at me anymore. And then another thought follows. I can invite Brock over, then he won't be mad at me either.

"Yes," I tell Hadley. She squeals with delight, and Rachel jumps up and down on her toes.

"Thank you, thank you, thank you, Heather!" Hadley reaches out and hugs me tight. I breathe in the hug, knowing she's happy with me again. She loves me again.

"I'm picking you up at 9 a.m. tomorrow, OK? I have Rachel's mom's number. I'll check in tonight," I tell her, though I'm not sure I will. Hopefully, I'll be too busy with Brock to let myself worry.

"Oh, there's my mom's car!" Rachel points to a black BMW in the car line and runs toward it. "Come on, Hadley!" she calls over her shoulder.

"OK, bye, Heather, love ya!" Hadley calls to me as she follows behind Rachel.

"Bye, Hadley-B—" I cut myself off before I can say the rest of her nickname. But she doesn't notice, she's already climbing into the backseat of the car.

Brock and I have sex on the couch, the kitchen counter, in the shower, and in the guest bed. If he was mad at me when he arrived, it only lasted the thirty seconds it took for me to push him onto the couch and jump on his lap. I'm always turned on by Brock, but feeling his hands on me here, where I work, feels wrong and dirty and turns me on even more.

Finally, too tired for another round, we lie naked against each other in bed, scrolling on our phones, when I notice the time—9 p.m.—Hadley's bedtime. I start to type out a text to Rachel's mom, just to check in and make sure the girls are at least in bed, though I know they won't be going to sleep anytime soon, when I remember the puppet show she was watching last night.

"Oh my god, Brock. I have to show you this weird show that Hadley was watching last night," I tell him, knowing he'll think it's just as weird as I do. He looks at me with raised eyebrows, curious. I close the unfinished text and pull up a search engine.

"It was like, Looney Louis or something," I say, as I type in everything that I can remember. The search "Looney Louis Puppet Show" corrects to *Lunatic Looey's Puppet Show*, and I click on the first link.

The link takes me to what appears to be a livestream, and I immediately recognize the style of the wooden marionettes dancing on my phone screen as the same I saw on the TV that Hadley was watching last night.

"Yeah, this is it," I say, and Brock leans in to see. The puppets aren't boy puppets like they were last night. Instead, they are little girl puppets. And this time, they appear to be in a bedroom, complete with a bed and a big, open window on the back wall.

The two puppets are sitting cross-legged on the floor, one with blond hair and one with chestnut hair with gold highlights that catches my attention. She's wearing a daisy print tank top.

"That's so weird," I say. "That one looks just like—"

"Hadley!" the blond puppet calls out in a nasally British

whine. "We're going to have so much fun tonight."

"Oh, shit, isn't that the name of the little girl you watch?" Brock mutters. I nod and sit up straight.

"Good thing my babysitter let me! She's such a cow." The Hadley puppet gestures wildly with her small wooden hands.

I grab the sheet and pull it over my bare breasts as if the puppets and puppeteer can see me as clearly as I can see them.

"Old, ugly Heather the Babysitter wouldn't know fun if it bit her on the ass." The Hadley puppet cocks her head to the side, and my jaw drops in shock. It's as if *she's* saying these words and not an adult man pulling the strings out of frame.

I feel a catch in my throat, like I can't breathe. I scan the screen for any clues that this is a joke on me somehow, but find nothing, just a cartoon eye in the corner with a number that is consistently growing, now at 11,546, suggesting that's how many people are currently watching. The comments that roll through on the bottom of the screen are coming and going too fast for me to read all of them, but the few I catch don't offer me any information. They read "Just kill them already," and "Make them pillow fight," and, most disturbing to me, "Kill the babysitter too."

"I'll show you how to have fun, Hadley," the puppeteer says for the blond marionette.

"Show me, Rachel. Show me, show me, show me!"

"This has to be some kind of a prank, right?" I say more to myself than to Brock.

"Maybe he uses the names of viewers. You said she likes this show," Brock says, and I exhale. Yes, of course, that's it. My fear shifts to anger. I'm livid with Hadley for being stupid enough to give a stranger on the internet so many personal details, and not just *her* details, but *mine* too. I feel a pang of guilt, knowing I should monitor what she's doing on her iPad more closely.

"Have you ever tried to fly?" the Rachel puppet asks the Hadley one.

"No, I haven't got any wings!"

"You don't need wings!" The Rachel puppet leads the Hadley puppet to the open window behind them.

"I don't understand. How am I meant to fly without wings?" The Hadley puppet stands on the windowsill, looking downward.

"Like this." The Rachel puppet gives the Hadley puppet a swift push, and Hadley falls out of frame with an ear-piercing scream. "Oh well! I guess Hadley-Bears can't fly," the Rachel puppet says to the camera.

"What the fuck…?" Brock mutters. "This shit is dark."

My throat closes up again, and the puppeteer pushes the bedroom set out of the frame. With a clattering of wood, he drops Hadley from above, leaving the puppet in a tangle of limbs and string as he squirts what appears to be ketchup from off screen, covering the puppet in a steady stream of blood-red goo until you can barely make out the body at all.

The image disappears, and my phone vibrates, causing me to jump. The words *Rachel Park's Mom Calling* replace the dead puppet, and I answer as soon as I register what's happening.

"Hello?" I ask urgently, jumping out of bed, realizing that I'm still naked and grabbing the sheet to cover my body in vain.

At first, there is silence on the other end. Then I hear a sharp, watery inhale.

"There's been an accident."

Independence Day

July 2nd

The summer sun scorched my skin when I stepped onto the sidewalk as Kevin and I walked out of city hall together, officially divorced. I brought my hand to my face to shield my eyes from the bright yellow daylight and prepared to say goodbye to my now ex-husband.

"Hey, I parked a few blocks away," he said. "Do you mind giving me a ride to my car?"

"Um, yeah, sure." I looked down at my phone, pulling up the Maps app. I had planned on getting lunch by myself at the deli across the street as a treat to my, now legally, single self, so I wasn't prepared to walk to my car, let alone with Kevin. "I parked in the garage on West Elm, so, um..." Typing the parking lot's address on my phone, I waited for directions to magically appear as they always did. I rarely ever drove downtown and still got turned around when I did.

"So to the left..." he said smugly. "I'm honestly worried about how you're managing without me, Olivia." He walked confidently toward the parking garage, and I followed.

"I've been doing well," I tried to say confidently, but my voice wavered, unprepared to talk to him. It's not like I was sad; I hadn't been for a while. Kevin and I had been separated for six months, which proved enough time to allow me to start living a relatively normal life without him. I had just hoped that after the judge declared us divorced, there would be no reason for us to talk to each other again. Ever.

I *had* been doing well, though I had to downsize immensely; I'd moved out of our three-bedroom home into a studio apartment I could still barely afford on my preschool teacher's salary. Unwilling to admit I needed his help, I didn't seek alimony or any other form of financial support. I wanted a clean break, with no monthly checks held over my head the way they had been for the four years of my marriage.

"I mean, you'd be wandering the streets, looking for your car if I hadn't asked you for a ride." I said nothing. Any melancholy I'd felt inside the courtroom had all but disappeared after spending less than five minutes alone with him.

"I wanted to let you know, now that the divorce is official, I'm going to ask Nelly to marry me."

"Oh, wow, that's soon," I said, though I wasn't surprised. Even though they'd only been dating for three months, Kevin wasted no time in posting on all social media accounts about how happy he was to finally find a "good, God-fearing woman." I wasn't offended by that. If anything, it reassured me that the divorce was the best course of action for us. Good and God-fearing, I was not. And until recently, I hadn't known that Kevin wanted me to be.

"She's already twenty-five and not getting any younger. And we want to have children." His words settled heavily in the air between us.

The choice to divorce was as mutual as it could have been. We got married when we were both twenty-four, and neither of us had a clear vision for the future. We were excited to figure it out together. Now, four years later, Kevin knew he wanted at least four children and a white picket fence. I still didn't know exactly what I wanted, but I knew it didn't include children.

I'd learned a lot in my five years as a preschool teacher—most importantly that I didn't want children. The hours of crying, potty accidents, and unrestrained snot had left me jaded and positive I didn't want it in my home.

The only people who wanted children less than I did were the parents of the children I taught. That was never more apparent than when I had to make a call to a parent to send a child home with a fever. Some parents begged me to keep their children at school so they didn't have to pick them up. I had to explain that I couldn't legally do that, and with an exasperated sigh, they'd agree to care for their sick child. I heard Kevin's voice in each one of those phone calls. It was so easy to picture him picking up the phone, frustrated with the disruption in his day, the same frustration I was met with when I called him to tell him that my car wouldn't start at work. "Great, another thing for me to deal with." Even if I *had* wanted children, I wouldn't have wanted to have children with him.

The catalyst for the divorce was my secret stash of birth control. One day, frustrated with my spending, Kevin decided to audit my purchases. That was when he'd found my twenty-dollar monthly subscription to ThePill.com, which I had done well to hide for a year.

"You're spending twenty dollars a month to murder our future children?" Kevin had recently rediscovered the religion he had lost during his liberal college years and subsequently believed he should spread his seed and reproduce as much and as quickly as possible. Hoping it was just a phase, like his passion for NASCAR or juice cleanses—both obsessions that lasted just under ten months until he grew bored and moved on to the next thing —I kept my head down and waited for it to pass. But this preoccupation stuck, to the detriment of our marriage.

It was then that we knew we weren't on the same page and most likely never would be.

"Well, I wish you the best," I said to Kevin when I pulled

up to his car to let him out.

"You, too, Olivia. Try to take care of yourself." He smiled sadly, and slammed my car door.

July 3rd

When I was twenty years old, I'd left my parent's house and moved in with Kevin. This was my first time living alone, and despite everything Kevin had told me, despite everything I believed to be true, I loved it.

My space may have drastically decreased, but so did my workload. Laundry that used to take me a full day to wash, dry, fold, and put away was done in a few hours. Dishes took no time at all, mostly because all I could afford to eat was Top Ramen and bologna sandwiches, which could be eaten with plastic forks and on disposable plates. And I could do whatever I wanted. I could fall asleep watching *Sex and the City* on my laptop in bed. I could eat a pack of Girl Scout Cookies in one sitting if I wanted to. No one was there to be bothered, to judge.

I was proud of myself and how well I was doing, how well I was taking care of myself. I may not have been thriving, but I was doing more than surviving. And I was finally believing I didn't need Kevin the way he always told me I did.

Until the bugs.

On the elementary school playground, there is always one little girl horrified by the pill bugs and worms that poke out of the soil on rainy days, the one who brave little boys terrorized with hands full of creepy crawlies, running after her to make her squirm and scream. I was that girl.

Bugs were repulsive to me—their speed, their stealth, their dozens of legs. It made me gag just to think about it. So Kevin was the designated bug squasher in our house. It became routine for him to hear me squeal from another room and appear with a shoe in his hand and searching eyes, ready to strike, ready to be the hero.

The first bug I saw in my new apartment was an ant

on my kitchen counter. I could handle an ant. I could ignore an ant. It was harder, though, to ignore the line of them on the same kitchen counter, all neatly and strategically headed toward the sugar bowl. After a deep breath and an internal pep talk, I opened the lid of the sugar bowl and found dozens of ants diving in and out of their sweet, white treasure. I closed the lid and walked away, trying my best to forget what I saw while simultaneously accepting I'd be drinking coffee without sugar from now on.

Then there was the cockroach. I was standing, eating Cheerios from a Styrofoam bowl. I still hadn't saved up enough for a kitchen table, and even if I had, I wasn't sure how a table, even a small table, would fit in my studio apartment kitchen. So my options were to eat in bed or standing up, and after spilling a bowl of cereal in bed a week earlier, I'd decided that any food eaten in a bowl should be eaten standing in the kitchen.

I felt the cockroach before I saw it. My bare foot tickled under his six legs, and I looked down just in time to see his black, flat body scurry over my big toe and run under the refrigerator.

I gagged, and the milk that I had yet to swallow dribbled from my mouth back into the bowl.

It went on like this, bugs appearing and disappearing just as quickly, from nooks and crannies around my apartment. I took the approach of ignoring the problem and hoping beyond all reasonable hope they would magically go away, that the bugs would find a better home and move out. Unsurprisingly, that didn't happen. They never left, only multiplied.

That night, Kevin proposed to Nellie. Even though I didn't follow him on any platforms, my friends still did. I was inundated with screenshots of his engagement announcement, along with supportive messages.

"HE'S ENGAGED?"

"Omg did you see this?"

"Olivia, omg, she's so ugly. wtf."

In the picture, Kevin stood next to Nelly, in a paisley

button up. The top two buttons were unbuttoned, revealing his blond chest hair and a wooden cross necklace. Nelly's frizzy, brown curls were a halo around her face, and she held her left hand up to her gummy smile, showing off a small green gem on a thick gold band. She was happy, almost manically so, her green eyes wide and wild with excitement under her oversized glasses.

After receiving the picture for the fourth time, my throat closed up, and what I thought for a second might be vomit turned out to be a waterfall of tears. I cried hard, letting out every tear I'd been subconsciously holding in since I'd first said, "This isn't going to work, is it?" and he'd said, "No, I don't think so."

Yes, it was a good thing we were divorced. Yes, he made me feel awful and incapable. But we were in love once. We'd said our vows and were happy to say them, happy to commit the rest of our lives to each other. That wasn't why I was crying, though. I was crying because I'd already forgotten what it felt like to love Kevin and what it felt like to be loved by him. Something I once promised to feel for as long as I lived was gone as soon as we decided to divorce. He was the biggest part of my life for so long, I'd figured there'd be a Kevin-shaped hole in my life when he was gone, but there wasn't, or if there was, it took no time at all to fill with the fun and freedom of being single. There was no forever, everything ends. That's why I cried.

It was true, too, for the daddy longlegs that crawled on the wall above my bed. I saw him scurrying on the white drywall, my vision still blurry with tears. I cringed at the thought of standing on my bed, whapping the wall with the nearest shoe, hearing his legs crack and bulbous body squish beneath the sole of my pink flip-flop. Then it occurred to me I didn't have to kill him. He would die soon without my help. Probably before he had the chance to do any damage to me or my tiny apartment.

"You can stay," I said to him. He stopped moving as if listening to me. "I'm going to bed," I said to the spider, to the cockroaches, to the ants, to all the creepy crawlies who may be listening. After I rolled over onto my stomach, I fell asleep.

I dreamed about bugs. Stink bugs, cockroaches, ants—all in bed with me. Mosquitoes, gnats, and flies buzzing around my ear, humming in harmony, "Thank you for letting us live."

I woke to a buzz from my phone, a text message from Kevin.

"I was showing Nelly our wedding video, and she wants the centerpieces. Can I come by and pick them up from you tomorrow?"

Our centerpieces were old books, stripped of their covers and tied in bundles with burlap. They took me and my four bridesmaids an entire weekend to make and were still in an open cardboard box by the front door. After I'd cut the box open while unpacking, I'd realized I had no idea what to do with them. It felt wrong to throw them out, and what seemed like such a good idea for our wedding was now a waste of space and books.

"You can have them," I typed back to Kevin and sent him my address. He replied with a thumbs-up emoji.

July 4

Kevin had never been to my apartment, and as I washed my hair in the shower, a pit of dread grew hot and heavy in my stomach. I imagined the smirk on his face when I opened the door and he surveyed my space in one glance. He would see a tower of cardboard boxes yet to be unpacked—there was no place to put the contents if I had. He would see the bare walls and outdated kitchen appliances. And there would be a comment about how I couldn't take care of myself. Because there always was.

In the shower, the water pooled around my ankles, and I groaned. I'd have to go out and buy Drano to pour down the shower drain today. I rinsed the shampoo from my hair and watched the white suds fall to the water and cling to the surface of my rising shower-pond.

My gaze was broken when I saw a silverfish scurry from behind the shower curtain liner into the pooling water. I jumped out of the shower, sopping wet, without a second thought. Wrapping a towel around me, I turned the water off. I backed away from the tub and saw another silverfish run from behind the toilet into the bathtub, and another and another. A line of them dove into my dirty bathwater. I was too mesmerized to act and, surprisingly, too fascinated to be disgusted.

After the tenth silverfish made the plunge, the line stopped. I crept forward slowly and cautiously to see if they were still under the water or if they'd escaped down the drain. Ten silverfish crawled up the side of the tub together, slowly, huddled around a wet, hairy mass the size of my fist. It was *my* hairy mass, the culmination of over a month of my chestnut brown hair that had gathered and tangled in the drain, blocking the water from flowing.

The silverfish worked slowly to drag the hairball out of the tub, and as they did, the bathwater slowly disappeared, able to drain once again without the blockage.

Under the fluorescent light of my bathroom, I saw for the first time how beautiful they were. The silver backs of the bugs caught the light, and their determination and teamwork were captivating, admirable.

"Thank you," I whispered as the ten workers left the hairball on the ledge of the tub and retreated in a line back to wherever they came from behind the toilet. I picked up the wet clump, plopped it into the toilet and flushed. I thought again that nothing lasts forever. Everything ends. It was just as true for disgust as it was for love.

I had no plans for the Fourth of July, but Kevin didn't need to know that. So I dressed in a strappy red dress that emphasized my cleavage and put on the brightest shade of red lipstick I owned. I wasn't dressing to impress him, or to remind him how much hotter I was than Nelly. It was to remind him I wasn't a good, godly woman, or whatever it was he had found in Nelly. I was the opposite, I was bad, devilish. And capable.

I smacked my freshly painted lips in the bathroom mirror and saw that a small, winged insect had landed on my reflection. I reached out, not to kill it or to shoo it, but to touch it. "Do you love me?" my reflection asked the gnat. He leaped from the mirror to my face, just above my lip, like a beautiful black beauty mark. "Of course you do."

The gnat stayed on my face when I left the bathroom. He stayed there as I plucked the box of wedding centerpieces from the pile of boxes. I opened the flaps and peered inside at the bundles of coverless books. They were kitschy and silly and something that may have been cute four years ago but seemed tacky now. No wonder Nelly liked them.

I grabbed the packing tape, but before I could use it, I saw movement among the books. I pushed the first bundle aside, and dozens of tiny spiders scattered. *Shit*, I thought. I can't give these to Kevin now. My phone vibrated on the linoleum floor. Kevin had sent just three letters, "OMW." He was on his way. I directed my attention back to the box of spider-infested books. "Shit," I said, aloud this time, gripping the sides of the box. Then the spiders climbed up my arms. It didn't hurt. It didn't tickle like I thought it would. I could barely feel the hundreds of legs now against my arms. Still, my skin grew goosebumps beneath them. I hadn't realized how hungry for touch I had been. The spiders didn't stop at my arms. They climbed my shoulders, neck, and cheeks, to my hair. I sat still, shivering beneath them, waiting to see what they'd do.

Then came the stink bugs, rushing from the screens of my open windows. And the cockroaches from under the refrigerator in the kitchen. Ants, ladybugs, daddy longlegs, mosquitoes, flies, all swarmed me, starting at my fingertips and rushing to the top of my head. This went on for what felt like hours, but when my phone buzzed again with another text message—"Parking"—I saw it had only been ten minutes since his last message. I brought my phone to my face and turned on the front camera to see myself, to see the bugs.

Their bodies piled on each other atop my head, creating a living, breathing, wriggling, writhing crown. "Let us help you." It was more of a vibration than a sound, and I felt it hum through every bone in my body. My beauty mark flitted his tiny, iridescent wings against my upper lip.

"OK." I exhaled, still admiring myself on the screen in my palm. I was more beautiful than I'd ever been, an insect queen in her insect crown. When I returned my attention back to the box, the tiny spiders descended my neck, shoulders, and arms, back into the books, but the rest of my servants stayed perched on my head.

"More," I said, and more, bigger spiders joined the box. When I was satisfied with the number of arachnids climbing over the centerpieces, I whispered, "Hide," and they did. They hid between bundles and under the bows of burlap. When I couldn't see any spiders at all, I closed the flaps and taped it shut. I stood gracefully, careful not to drop my crown, but I didn't have to worry—it moved with me. It swayed and breathed with me. It was a part of me.

Two loud pounds sounded against my apartment door. *Knock, knock.*

"Come in," I buzzed, and he did.

Megan Mary Moore is a writer working in Cincinnati and living in a fairy princess fever dream. She is the author of the poetry collections To Daughter a Devil (Unsolicited Press, 2023) and And Aphrodite Laughs (Milk & Cake Press, 2023) . Her debut novel, The Girl in the Pipes is forthcoming with Unsolicited Press. She holds an MFA in poetry from Miami University.

You can find her on Instagram @meganmarymoore

Vince the Variant
Part 1

Where should I begin? I am a vampire, but I am not what you would expect. I am what some would call a *variant*. When most think of vampires, they imagine them in a world of fiction, but just like stereotypes, they exist for a reason. Let's get real. The number of cultures with their own myths about vampires that are oddly similar in description is uncanny, and still, we've managed to stay within the realm of fantasy. Great for our survival…sometimes. But I'll get into that later.

I am a vampire, but I am repulsed by blood. *Ugh*! It makes me gag just thinking about it. Anyways, a vampire repulsed by blood. I know, kind of seems to miss the point. There are a few different variant vampires who have popped up throughout history, and some died off swiftly depending upon their food source and what sort of availabilities were around. But my particular gene is a bit odd, I recognize. I am a fashionista in the realest sense. I am obsessed by it, but I also need it to not only live but to thrive.

Humans are simple in what fuels them, so it's obvious why it's so hard for them to fathom a food source not being ingested specifically. Maybe that's why the lore of blood-sucking vampires is the only one that continues to stick in more ways than one. They exist, and sometimes really give the rest of us a bad name, on top of limiting the acceptance of our social settings. They feel our gene dampens the likelihood of containing our existence into myths and folklore, and I don't blame them since I have had some extremely close calls. I've become a bit of a recluse these days.

I have fed on blood as a sort of desperation when bad fashion is around me when I am starving. Those were low times, and I wondered if I was doomed, as some of my late ancestors—including Petro—who lived part of his prime in Kansas until an early death in the 1980s. Just thinking about that era of fashion, I shudder about how he must have struggled. Don't get me wrong, there were some gems in the 1980s, but not too many. Plus, location, location, location! It really is everything, and he never seemed interested in moving to a different place. It was as if he was meant to be doomed. What a tragedy.

It's 2025, and I am quite impressed with humans these days. They lean toward practicality in a lot of their fashion, without sacrificing too much of what makes fashion art. I crave both men's and women's fashion. Love the floral dresses coming up this season. Was bothered the Pantone color this year is Mocha Mousse. But with my love of suits and bow ties, I can really run with this. While I enjoy both genders' clothing, I consider my style a cross between effortless elegance and tradition meets innovation. I thrive in slim-fit suits with bow ties or ties, and on other days, I enjoy slim jackets with short lapels to add a bit of dressiness in a simple and tasteful way. But then, there are the billowy fabrics on coats and trousers to add comfort and ease to my sleek wardrobe, allowing me to strut. On the flip side, what is it about plaids that are both generic and yet so delicious looking in the way they can be tailored with an added flair?

There was another ancestor of ours, Vanessa, who lived during the Victorian era in England. She thrived. What a time to be alive! She almost exposed our species because of her recklessness, which is not hard to do with our particular gene. She came from aristocrats and had quite the appetite! From the numerous embroideries and decorations and petticoats. They could rarely contain her from causing screams in the streets. She was *put down*, as one would say, by her family. They tried to restrain her for a short stint, but Vanessa was clever in her attempts to indulge herself. Thus, they gave her no choice but to be beheaded.

I feel like I should give a bit more history on what my gene is and how we are able to be. I mean, blood vampires are not born that way, so how am I able to exist? Do I just suddenly reject blood? Now that would be interesting, wouldn't it? Oh, how traumatic! In most myths of vampires it's a big thing, because of the whole death thing, that vampires cannot create life. In most cases, no, but on the rare occasion, a variant is created. Maybe that is nature's way of figuring out a loophole to this whole blood thing. But this is part of my story.

My parents, Regina and Ezra, were blood vampires for centuries and could consummate easily. Well, shortly after a wild, extravagant party and a passionate night, my mother was pregnant. It's not unheard of, but they were concerned, wondering what type of variant I would be. Since creating life from something that is supposed to be sort of dead is a bit unnatural, giving birth really just depends on the baby and the food source around it. I am thirty-two and it's 2025, and since I crave fashion, as you can imagine, I was feeling the scrumptious urge to consume pretty quickly. My parents were both fashionable, wealthy, and blended in. It took me only four months to shove my way out. For a while, my parents contained me by bringing people they found irresistible for feeding, ensuring the fashion I craved was part of those poor humans' wardrobes.

I have heard the story about my first noticeable victim too many times to count (the day they figured out my gene). I was only a few days old and rejecting blood, and I saw a shiny shoe when I was out with my mother that grabbed my attention. My eyes lit up while I was in her arms, and when I reached out, there was a sort of *vroom* and *pop* sound. Then that baby's shoe was on my foot, and I was happy and laughing. She rushed away as another confused mother looked for her baby's shoe.

In my teenage years, my parents' patience was constantly tried, and eventually, they moved away, concerned I would out them with my impulses. Their bloodlust can be contained in the night and the dark corners of the world, where mine thrives in the light. Yes, I can see in the night, and most other similar abilities my parents and "normal" vampires have. This includes abilities such as strength, speed, and charm, but the best fashion tends to be in places where people can show off their styles, their art, and it's delicious! Occasionally, I'll get a letter on their updates across the globe. They stopped telling me their stationary locations because, at sixteen, I started looking for them, but at twenty-four, I gave up and gave them their peace.

Most days now, I try to be like my blood-sucking family members and lurk in the dark by going to clubs with A-listers. I have to be careful, though. It's risky targeting celebrities. There's nothing more awkward than a naked or partially clothed famous person confused or screaming or staring at me among all the paparazzi snapping constantly. I mean, it's blatant who the culprit is. Oh yes, I have skipped a few parts.

Unlike my blood-sucking cousins, in order for me to feed, when I see fashion that just gets me and I have to have it, it violently rips off someone's body and goes right onto me in the most satisfying way. But that individual is left without, and as you can imagine, if I have their clothes on in front of them, shock, confusion, fear, and all the above happen pretty quickly. So, depending on the outfit, they end up naked or partially clothed.

Over the years, I have really honed my style. The problem with being a fashionista variant is that when I see bad, appalling, or even mediocre clothes, it frustrates and often angers me. I have to be careful where I am walking. I've killed a few because of my passionate disgust for outfits. Sometimes, I forget my strengths. That's when I have to really finish the job, though I do hate killing.

Early on, my parents tried to get me into blood, and much to their dismay, I threw it up immediately and screamed. I had continuously frustrated parents who did not know how to deal with this new being who had literally fallen into Regina's womb. Talk about being misunderstood! I have tried blood over the years when I am really lacking sustenance, and I cannot manage to get it down without vomiting violently. Then I end up having to kill the horrified people in different ways, and then I hit more of a low and feel bad about killing them. I never possessed the passion for death that my other family members thrive on. Mostly, I just feel guilty. I don't want to disrupt humans. I actually kind of like them and have tried to befriend some, and that just gets awkward and sometimes is worse. They cannot know about me. I've tried with those who are mediocre in their fashion tastes, but then I get bored with them quickly and frustrated by their lack of interest in improving their fashion. And why would I want them to improve, because then I would be taking from them on the regular? But then, the humans I tried to befriend who had great fashion were just confused all the time, especially with my body language and my lowered head. I did not want to take from them, even though I wanted to consume them. I wanted to see their beautiful selves in their beautiful clothes and ravage them.

I need fashion to survive, but to survive, I need to be unknown. A constant conundrum. Constantly alone. Why can't Mother Nature create pairs of this gene? Someone I could share my life with? Could there be a magnetic force that pulled us together?

I have been feeling conflicted lately, in hiding since my last unintentional kill. But with Easter coming up and one of the biggest fashion shows of the year arriving in my city a few months before ...*squeal*! I cannot contain both my excitement and my fear! I have to be out there. Runway! Easter! Full of delectable pastels, floral prints everywhere. New and innovative fashion, revealing what will soon make its way to the streets of New York. I learned from my previous horror show that I can no longer appear at fashion shows, but I do love when they come to my city. I enjoy those gearing up for the show, presenting themselves in all of their best and fabulous fashions, walking on a silver platter for me to consume in the streets.

The "horror" show at Fendi's ninetieth anniversary fashion show in Paris with the main event at the Trevi Fountain in Rome.

It was a time when I thought I could control my appetites at the ripe age of twenty-three (what was I thinking?), and it was a celebration of Fendi's Fall 2016 Couture collection (which was also their ninetieth anniversary and Karl Lagerfeld's fiftieth year at the house) with the main event having the Trevi Fountain as the backdrop. Imagine models walking on a transparent plexiglass runway over the Trevi Fountain's shallow pool to look as if they were walking on water. Obviously, I couldn't miss it, and I had been working on using what therapists like to call cognitive behavior therapy to help control my cravings and impulses and center myself. As a fashion connoisseur, I don't have to inhale every piece. I also spent a good part of the year in Central Park, working on controlling my appetites and testing myself on items of clothing that both repulsed and excited me to prepare for this upcoming show. NYC is full of diversity in fashion, and that can be overwhelming in both directions. I started out only being able to sit in the park for a few minutes at a time, and I only accidentally killed maybe five people in eight months. Sounds like a lot, and it is a lot when you hate yourself for killing and despise hurting others, but compared to my blood-sucking family members and my nature, five in eight months is low, or at least that's what I told myself. I genuinely thought I could do it…silly me, but here's what happened.

I follow all the best fashion magazines (*Vogue, Harper's Bazaar, L'Officiel, Marie Claire, GQ, Vanity Fair, etc.*), so between that and social media, I thrive on staying on the up and up with what's happening in fashion and where. I have to be careful, as I can get quite lost in the sources and be gone for days, binging through the magazines and pictures. But they're not real, and they don't feed me. All of my sources were talking about this particular show, *Legends and Fairytales*, for a solid year before it happened, and I needed to see it!

July 7 came fast, but I was ready. I flew into Paris a few days early and booked a luxury hotel nearby to treat myself. But it wasn't too close, in case something happened. Since I had been working on restraining myself the last year, I had focused on only stealing what was necessary to survive, and I'd also given back. I come from money, so I left my "victims" with more than what they paid for those items. It gives me a thrill to take from others instead of simply selecting items from the rack. So, with my more disciplined meal routine, times were hard. Restraint is *not* exciting.

I thought it would be fitting for my species, and the theme of the show, to go sleek, stylish, polished, and elegant, but not too flashy so I could blend in. Impress as I pretended to walk like a human. And since the theme of the show was *Legends and Fairytales*, I wanted a touch of fun in my outfit. I wanted to glide by, as one can, pretending to be human, and for them to admire and then forget about me.

I was at a good place in my life, managing my impulses, and I was putting this fashion show to the test. To really show off to those who didn't think I could survive this gene, if I was being serious. *Oh*, the many outfits I could have worn, but this was a show, and I wanted to be part of the glamour, the suspense, and the story. I was ready to eat it up. Figuratively, of course!

I started with a pair of these fitted leather pants to show that I could be stylish, yet elegant, for this whimsical show. Next, I went with a pale rose pink button-up. Wearing a white button-up would be a little too bright for this celebration of fashion. I added a fitted deep purple and red-wine colored vest with five prominent buttons down the middle. I chose the same color purple and red-wine patterned tie, with circles and diamonds in various shades to complement the deep, dark suit colors. A bit of an eye-catcher, while still blending in with the suit. On the left side pocket, I added a square handkerchief folded in a sort of side butterfly, with slightly more brownish-red tones to deep purple to stand out just slightly more than the tie in a balanced way. To top off the outfit, I added my suit jacket, which was the same color and style as the vest, and kept that open to view the five uniform buttons in the middle. Footwear is just as important as the suit. I went with a caramel Wingtip, and for those who are unclear with that name, they are also known as brogues. Stylish, made of leather, and simple, they gave a pop to my mostly dark aesthetic. For an edge and an air to my stature, but not revealing my weaknesses of struggle, I added a pair of sleek, slightly rectangular with a hint of chunkiness, black Ray-Bans. Normally, I am a fan of their classic style, but I picked these off a tourist (not to worry, I did not snatch from their face, just the shirt they were hanging off). I appreciated their modern edginess in a classic style. Sunglasses are essential for me because I can look down while seeming as if I am staring into a soul but not taking. A level and an air of confidence. Sleek and bold and comfortable, and ready to fill my fantasies while also proving I could reel in my impulses.

Part of the ticket to the show included chartered planes to transport guests from the couture shows in Paris to the main event in Rome, and then, of course, there was the after dinner and concert by the Italian soloist Anna Tifu and fourteen musicians from the Academia Nazionale di Santa Cecilia. I refrained from the Paris couture show, as I wanted to see the main event and not push my luck too much with doing all of them. Instead, I enjoyed fashion in the streets of Paris, adding a few thrills for meals to make sure I got it out of my system before the main event. So, naturally, there was no way the charter plane was doable for me for obvious reasons. That would be pushing it a bit, so I used my skills of speed and endurance to make my way to the Trevi Fountain and snuck in as if I had been on the charter. Before the show began, I felt the anticipation of excitement growing around me and smelled it on all of them as I casually and quietly glided by each person. The view of the fountain set as the stage looked surreal. Butterflies just thinking about it! Plus, there were the intricate details of the Trevi Fountain with multiple sculptures, including Oceanus, the god of water on a chariot, pulled in by seahorses projecting outward from the stone presenting the fountain of water. The stage was its own performance. So seeing it in front of the fountain with a show about to start at night was delightfully magical. Let alone the history of what it meant to toss coins into the fountain to pay the deities in charge.

Guests sat around the stage, which wrapped around the fountain. I intentionally picked a seat near a back corner to avoid attention and give myself a quick getaway should anything happen. I spent the time before the show walking by and admiring the various styles of the high-profile guests. As I lurked and glided between each section surrounding the stage, the crowd became more and more prominent in finding their seats. That's when I smelled a sort of glam scent and peered to my left and saw a gem, glittered out like a stylish fairy princess. We locked eyes, and I nodded in approval.

It became time for everyone to be seated, and the show began. I was already proud of myself for simply being an admirer and not a taker. Models walked out, and it was already fabulous! Each had their hair curled into tight ringlets tied partway up in various pastel ribbons to add to the storyline. There were bell sleeves, empire waists, floral details in the most intricate and satisfying way, delicate, thin lacy dresses, and crocheted dresses embroidered with mink and fringed leather. There were beautifully crafted boot heels in colors that both popped and paired well with each dress as its synced partner. The seating arrangement made it harder for most guests to appreciate the intricate details of the art displayed on the dresses, but with my being a vampire, I saw every detail and was giddy. Forty-six models with forty-six looks that captivated in individual stories. Still, no one was afraid of me, and I kept my composure. A bit sweaty, with a few dresses that really gripped me, but I was doing it. I was controlling my appetites.

Then, the end of the show happened, and all forty-six models came out on stage at once. I was ravenous and drooling. I let down my guard and tipped my sunglasses to really appreciate my view, and that is when it happened. When the screaming started. Twenty of the forty-six pieces I viewed, I craved, and when I admitted my craving, dresses and jackets and heels flew off bodies and into my direction. Heads turned, confusion unfolded, and I had half of several items clinging from my body as I tried to escape as quickly as possible while I consumed like a glutton. It was so embarrassing and satisfying! Needless to say, I'd ruined a show I'd wanted to see for a year because I couldn't help myself. I had to consume, and I was full for days. I hid after that, afraid to view the news. Did anyone see me? Was there going to be a knock at the door from my family? Was this going to be it? The end of my rope. Nine years later, I have steered clear of shows like that. Learned my lesson, and now spend my days hunting in less conspicuous ways.

I walk around eager with anticipation to take in all the delicious sights and see if I can contain myself. Sunny days are the best because humans put on their finest to frolic in the sun. I am enjoying the lovely sunshine on this breezy spring day, two days before Easter, when I see it. It is a pale rose twill slim-fit suit with an even softer pink button-up, a black tie, and a black-and-gold belt that pop in just the right way with a pair of black eel chain loafers without socks, attached to a new owner walking out of Tom Ford. It is mesmerizing and perfect for this beautiful day! I need it. After a quick scope of my surroundings, and with it not being busy with an alley just around the corner, I grab him and ravage him until the suit is perfectly and satisfyingly on my body. I sigh in satisfaction and disappear quickly before he can tell what has happened. I feel full and great until I look back in my quick escape and see his confused, distraught face. He wouldn't have seen me, but I imagine having your clothes ripped from you is not a good feeling. I left him in boxer briefs with his bags full of his previous clothes, so he wasn't at a total loss. I take a stroll through the streets, full and happy.

As I speed through the city enjoying my new suit matching this lovely sunshine, I glance at myself in a mirror and go back to admire it and notice it is wrinkled! *Does everything I own get wrinkled after I move at my true speed?* This is upsetting news. I smooth the suit and walk normally and check myself again in the mirror. My shirt and jacket are fine. I decide to take a quick run through the city and come back, and it is wrinkled again. So now, this gene of mine has me in more distress.

Vince began trying to figure out how to move at a fast pace and still keep his clothes in impeccable design and shape. What felt like forever to him, because of frustration, in reality, only took a few minutes. He found a new gait with his vampire speed that would not negatively affect his wardrobe and ultimately maintain his model-like appearance.

As I continue on my walk, I see her. The most beautiful and different creature I've ever seen. Dainty, yet fierce in the way she holds herself. Curiosity has covered her, and she seems to be entertained as she looks for something. No one signifies noticing her as she moves impossibly fast and still at the same time. She is wide-eyed and in awe of the world around her that doesn't seem to notice she exists. *Am I imagining things? I need to know her.*

Vince didn't realize this was the first time he'd never been interested in someone's wardrobe, but instead, in who they were. It was a magnetic pull, something he'd never experienced before. Different from the obsessive pulls he felt when reeling in those delicious meals off their bodies.

She is frolicking about in a blend of dancing and walking, mesmerized by everything she observes. She doesn't know that I am watching her, or so I think. That I am captivated by her. That I feel I have to know her. The sun is high, and the streets are full of fashion swirling around. *How can I approach her?* I want to follow her, but the streets are busier than normal, and I do not trust myself. I have to know her… I have to talk to her. To smell her … *Who is she?*

This magnificent creature is moving farther away, so I risk seeing where she goes. I try not to make it obvious that I'm following her, but suddenly, she disappears. A panic rises in my chest. I no longer care about my hunger, but instead, feel alone once again. Suddenly, I feel a light breeze flow past me and hear the sweetest voice speak, "There you are!" I turn around, and she is in front of me, smiling.

I say, "Do we know each other?"

She laughs. "We do, and you'll see." When she takes my hand and walks ahead of me, leading me, I swear I saw a second head staring at me, and then we are off.

Jane of Two
Part 2

Cascade mountain views exploit themselves in hopes that we genuinely desire to peer into them. To really see them. Their voices carry over and through horizons as we get lost in translation to define what is bestowed upon us, not just with our eyes, but with all senses. They exhibit the pleading desire for us to pause and gawk at their beauty and to truly crave it. Call it survival instincts embedded deep within their surrounding kingdoms.

Shadowy mists lurk poetically, hoping to lure you into realms of discovery. Hidden treasurers await the curious and eager just as much as the stubborn and bored. They risk being forgotten as we set up prisms, barricading ourselves away from their delectable views, giving us delusions that we are living in paradise as our walls mimic natural beauty, but instead, continue to isolate us within our own prisons.

Dust and moisture move and sway, drizzle and dance in their own music videos for all to see. Thunder and lightning storms reign sharply to remind the lost of their power and might, hoping fear will pull in the rebellious and challenge them into an awaited fight to prove who is king.

Occasionally, we are reminded of these majestic giants we use in folklore with pictures and trips telling of their strengths and lessons, knowing that when we are given the chance to peer at their mightiness, we cannot help but only be in awe.

Solstices speak in and out of realms twice a year, showcasing their intense beauty, hoping to engage with us as we flow together. Stillness and chaos interchanging. We've constantly come to worship those markers designed for such things.

We, in our rebellious need to conquer, see their tops and hurdles as a desire to triumph over them to give ourselves worth, and they seduce with excitement. Our eyes betray us in our appetites for thinking we could be invincible.

In their gates at the beginning, delicate life peeks through the ground and into the trees. Wildlife treads softly, leaning into gossip from the birds of a stranger and a potential enemy moving in. Secret lives of the wild are exposed only to those willing to become bored by the birds, those not tricked into thinking life is back to its regular scheduled programming.

The cycle of life and death more prominently portrayed, even though life exudes fervently. For every discovery of death, it seems almost tenfold the life pushing through and reclaiming its power.

Colors reign supreme, curated in instinctual galleries captivating eyes with wonder, allowing *us* to recreate its magic! Soft and rough intertwine, naming texture as its ally as more life moves in. So many worlds within this great kingdom, living and moving as one. Fascinated by kingdoms within kingdoms, all intertwined within each other, unaware of what they provide one another. Or maybe, they know. Maybe they are all aware of how their ecosystems move forces of nature in constant.

I stumble upon a lone tree engaging with the rocks as the falling water dances upon its source, creating more pleasure to the naked eye. Creating purpose for what seems like it's waiting to die, but instead, is dormant, dressed in winter and adding color to its rough counterparts. A purpose in and of itself. To simply be. Its roots pulling from an unlabeled water source to retain strength for when its purpose is revitalized for the new that will come.

As I move slightly uphill on this massive playground, the stillness of my surroundings gives my senses an eerie feeling. So much life, holding such silence as I crunch on top of many tiny worlds, unaware of what I may be disrupting or contributing to. The trees are scattered in their own uniform way. A calm army at attention as I weave through, seeing how far I can go. Inconsistencies among these soldiers in uniform take nothing away from what they've seen and lived. In fact, it gives more to their ghastly, strong, and calm figures as other worlds crawl up and mold with them, adding character and individuality.

Losing track of the time that has passed from my deep infatuation into exploration, I turn to look and realize I have already made it to a peak overlooking the many other kingdoms in view. This propels more desire to continue and forget the time I am spending away from my known. Being seduced and pulled in my intrigue, I still prepare myself for when night falls and different types of magic show themselves to me. Until then, I play with wonder and follow the sun into an unknown.

On this adventure, I tell myself to engage only with senses given to me at birth. Catching continuous panoramic views with just my naked eye has me wishing I did not negotiate with those kings to only intake. The desire to share and show hits deep into my core. *How many have seen what I have seen and will see as it is now?* I wonder. I increase my speed as the steepness creeps in. To fully perceive these worlds around me, I have allowed myself to retain a normal walking pace. I take in a breath of fresh air and close my eyes as I contemplate how destruction unfolds so much life. Powerhouses, known to us as volcanoes, spit fire on their time clocks in a rage of destruction and cleansing of those kingdoms depending to start anew, wiping out all. As a predator, I understand the need to take, but in my taking, I rarely give back like this current kingdom does.

I'm surrounded by tall grasses and wildflowers reaching

for the sun, eagerly shedding their scents in hopes they will be received and celebrated. I notice the sun is setting, and I know things will change. I am looking forward to seeing what befalls my eyes in the moonlight.

After I go over the side of the next ridge in the moonlight, I notice it. It's fast. Almost too fast. Definitely too fast for the normal naked eye. Once I glimpse what it might be, it suddenly disappears, and all is calm in the forest once again.

I don't feel threatened, and it had been following me for a few hours. I hit an incline again, my gaze toward the moonlight, and get a closer look. It sort of looks like a dust of color, surrounded by twinkling bees. As I lock eyes with it and focus, I realize it is some sort of being that appears like a woman with two heads and moving so fast in one place to mask itself from eyesight. I have always been able to move quickly and see things most cannot.

In the few moments of getting it, or her, into focus, I raise my voice and say, "Hello! I can see you. Why have you been following me?" It suddenly darkens again, and for a moment, there is nothing. When I think she is gone, I feel a quick breeze hit me, and a dash of colors whirl at me and around me. In a flash, she is in front of me.

A quick laugh and a smile, and she sticks her hand out and says, "We are Jane." I pause, and she speaks again. "Did I get it wrong? Is handshaking not customary for you?" I reach out, unsure whether to trust this creature before me.

We shake, and I introduce myself. "Hello, Jane. I am Vince." She seems delighted and does a quick leap into the air in satisfaction.

I ask her, "Where did you come from? Do you live here? What are you?"

Jane sits and pats the ground next to them and said, "They've called me by many names throughout time. They've called me Faerie because of how I move in between worlds and what they see when they occasionally glimpse a view of me or how I seem to flutter and shimmer in place. How I dance and giggle and play. They've called me Muse because of the inspiration I have given them. They've called me Fate because of some of the roles I have filled throughout history, how I see the world and explain to those willing to listen. They've called me Nymph because of my beauty, my freeness in nature. They've called me Witch because of what I can produce in an instance. I am here, and I am simply Jane." After she speaks, she stares at me wide-eyed, and I feel like I have known her my whole life.

She smiles and says, "Now that's out of the way, before you came, I was contemplating a new adventure on my annual hobby. Would you like to see what I have been up to the last couple of years?"

Unknowing what will happen next, I am altogether comfortable and intrigued by this being, so I reply, "Why not?" She takes my hand and begins.

It was then Jane explained her third annual yearly event of picking a time and a big city around a day of celebration and firebombs in the sky. She found it fascinating the way she could fly without her normal methods and observe, play, and try to figure them out. Them being humans.

I have been fascinated by bicycles since their invention and throughout their evolution. About five years ago, I found myself in the year of 1817 in Germany, after lurking in and around different parts of the world, and it was then I noticed this man by the name of Karl von Drais creating something with two wheels with brass bushings within the wheel bearings, iron-shod wheels, a rear-wheel brake, a wooden frame, and a cushioned seat. I observed him and learned that in order to propel it, one must use their feet by pushing off the ground, which caused the wheels to turn and made it faster for humans to move without the help of horses. I was hooked from then on and delighted by this creation!

Popping in during different time periods, I continued observing the evolution to see how this would evolve. From the 1820s to the 1850s, other designers started adding more wheels, adding pedals, treadles, and hand cranks, but none stuck because of a lack of function. Shortly after, I got bored and returned to other adventures and avenues, as I liked to mix up my hobbies and sort of forgot about the bicycle. On one of my whims about three years ago, I found myself in Scotland in the 1800s, where the Industrial Revolution was well on its way and Scotland was making a name for itself in innovation. I found myself specifically in the 1840s, and as I walked down the street in Glasgow, I noticed a bicycle ride past me, which would later be reported in a traffic accident. But this was different, it moved faster. I leaped farther through time to see where this small invention would be carried next and found myself following up through time and in different countries for a solid year. I witnessed the bicycle go from a wooden frame to two pieces of cast iron bolted together in France to a single-piece frame made of wrought iron, which made the invention much more durable. That's when, as they like to call it, the "bicycle craze" began. It was fun observing the modifications to what was originally such a simple design. After spending a year as an observer, hopping around in time to see its evolution, I decided to take a more active approach to the bicycle and ride it. I needed to determine which time period to explore first for the best experience.

After much thought and observation, I selected the year 1885 in the United States of America, and chose the American Star Bicycle that was invented by G. W. Pressey in New Jersey. It was odd-looking, with a large back wheel and a smaller one in the front to stop the bicycle from tipping, supposedly. The handlebars and seat were placed near the larger wheel, and it had a more modern approach by using a treadle instead of a crank to get the bicycle moving. The seat was still a cushion, and so, that was the experience I chose after all of those years. I had seen a new prototype enter that completely changed the style, but I wanted to see what riding the uneven wheels was like.

It was the beginning of July, and I was hearing a lot of buzz around their annual celebration of independence. So I planned it out. It was harder than anticipated, purchasing one of these bicycles, but I wanted to remain honest. I stayed on the East Coast and blended in. Women were wearing these impossible dresses, and their lack of practicality was offensive at best, so I found some trousers popular of the day. They were formal, three-piece tailored suits, with a top hat or bowler hat, and I went with the bowler hat to prevent drawing too much attention to my riding. I stayed in Jersey City and planned to start from one end of the city and ride to the other, while firebombs painted the sky. Anticipation grew, and I saw and felt the excitement on their faces as they placed themselves on blankets near the water and stood or sat ready to witness their country's expression of freedom and independence. The firebombs started as soon as the sun set, and that's when I started my ride. It was awkward at first, but I was determined to figure it out and make my way through the city. It was just as fun as I had observed, witnessed, and hoped. After that year, I decided to make it a tradition and pick another time period of the evolving bicycle and the independence celebration.

In my second year, I went much forward this time, having contemplated the 1950s and 1960s, but then I thought, *What about even more advanced bicycles than those of that period?* The bicycles in the '50s and '60s seemed faster and better than the one I rode a bit awkwardly in 1885, but I wanted to see how I could fly on the ground. So, I picked the mid-1990s grunge style. I chose the trick bike, as they liked to call it.

Every year, Jane tried a different bicycle, and found she became enamored with what's known as the ten-speed in her recent observations. She felt she could really "fly," groove, and shift through angles easily. She also liked to pick a new style every year that humans boasted about being fashionable.

After Jane described to me how she started her hobby, she opened a small window to show me what it would be like. I could see it clear as day! It was as if I was her and yet was watching her.

This year, she found a style they pegged as "grunge." She wore sneakers, as they called them, which were both comfortable and restricting, and she tried to find the functionality. Since the style she went with was catered to a grittier look, she went with a different bike this year, what's known as the "trick bike."

Times had evolved to playing music on a device called the radio, and it blared on loudspeakers synced with the firebombs in the sky. *More evolving art*! Jane loved continuing through Jersey City as she had during her first experiment on a bicycle in 1885. It was a thick and hot July, and she started on the east side of the city once the music began playing, enjoying weaving slowly and then speeding up to get the feel of the wind hitting her. Crowds had grown larger than before, with more people interested, there to see this representation of independence and freedom. So she stayed a bit on the outskirts to not be noticed easily nor run into anyone. Typically, music and fireworks took anywhere between fifteen and twenty-five minutes to get through, and Jane figured it typically takes thirty to forty-five minutes to bike from the east to the west side of Jersey City. She was determined to prove she would accomplish this goal before the end of the music and the fireworks.

Jane rode her bike rapidly. It was exhilarating, different from what she was used to. Nights like this were safest near the ground. "They love seeing fire in the skies!" Jane thought with fascination. Humans would spend hours, traveling in lengths to gather and gawk in awe at the different colors exploding, without a care for anything else around them nor any consequences or outcomes that may occur. It was all about how thrilled they felt at that moment.

She found it fascinating. She didn't come to the city often, but loved to take her chosen bike and "fly" with wheels to the ground, grinding. It was her third yearly adventure saturating herself in "their" world. She loved to mimic them and see how they viewed the world so closely to the ground.

Boom!Boom! It took some time getting used to those loud sounds. Every boom cultivated cheers throughout the city. Music and dancing occurring simultaneously. Jane still hadn't figured out the why behind the one-day event, something to do with independence. She never cared to delve too deep into their whys. She steered clear of them because of her differences and the fact that they were unaware of her existence. Jane tried to make herself as much of an invisible spectator to this once-a-year celebration of magic as she could.

With her special skills, she illuminated in a way that was both mesmerizing and unnoticeable to the common eye. Although she stayed glued to the bike in the grounding sort of way it's meant to be, she twirled in speed and grace with both careless velocity and speed, along with strategic steadiness, to go unnoticed.

Bam!Swoosh! "Sorry about that! I haven't quite figured out how to share things with others and bring them back without a bit of a knock," Jane pronounced. "After hearing of my adventures, would you like to join me in the far future to see where bicycles have evolved and if they still exist? I know a place that brings in all sorts from all over the galaxies. It's a bit of a dive, but many characters come through, and one of them is bound to have a sort of bicycle. Humans are obsessed, just as I am. I know we are stepping away from these celebrations, but I am curious as to where they go."

Vince is reeling with excitement for this new venture, but also to see potential fashion discoveries. He enjoys Jane's disclosure of the fashions of each time period. She doesn't seem bothered by who he was and what he needed to thrive. Vince holds out his hand and says, "Let's go!" And in an instant, they land in a desert, standing in front of a dusty large sort of dive bar in the middle of nowhere. Vince looks at Jane as she smiles and leaps in excitement. "I've peered in here a few times, and I wonder how they all get here. And I think there might be a bicycle around, or something new."

"They?" Vince says, looking at the deserted bar. They step inside, and no one is there. There are wooden chairs everywhere in a circumference around a large bar in the center of the room.

Vince looks at her again, and she smiles and says, "Just wait, you'll see."

After what feels like an hour, a few different beings trickle in with various looks and styles, and one sits at the bar. He has a steampunk look to him, with white-and-silver hair sticking up. He orders a colorful drink and, seeming to notice us from across the room, a huge smile crosses his face. I wave, but he seems like he is in a trance. Jane speaks up and says, "He's reminiscing of days past."

"What a day!" thought Mitra. He had been traveling for quite some time on his hoverboard and decided to stop at the local bar. Mitra stepped off his board and tapped the side button so it folded quickly and neatly into the size of a ring box, and he slipped it into his pocket and walked into the dirty, dusty desert dive named You Are Here. He always found it a strange name for a bar in the middle of nowhere, but this was a surprising hot spot, and central to everywhere you needed to go. When he walked inside, he scanned the room and briefly saw bodies on the other side. He made a beeline for the corner bar, his favorite spot when it was available. The bartender, as always, came out of nowhere, asking what he wanted to drink. Since it was a hot day and he wanted something refreshing, he decided on a tequila sunrise. Seems like an odd choice for a bar in the middle of nowhere, but they made everything and nothing.

Mitra sipped his drink and scanned the room. As

he looked closer at the bodies on the other side of the bar, he noticed the oddity of the couple sitting there. Odd was a loose term, since most beings that graced this bar were from everywhere and anywhere. He noticed the one facing toward him as a pale face. "Hmm, I haven't seen a pale face in a long time. What is one of them doing here of all places in the middle of the day?" he thought. Then he noticed a petite being next to him who radiated warmth and cheer, who seemed to see him without facing him. They laughed and flowed together, and it reminded him of a memory he had forgotten.

He was back in India, celebrating the Hindu holiday Holi and color play, and that's when he realized he knew her in a simpler time. Wait, was she…?

I was back home, and everyone was gearing up for this special holiday, neighbors and family, gathering together to share in color play. Everyone dressed in white linens, various colors of chalk powder set aside for the big moment. They started with a big meal, full of laughter and game plans for adventure at each door. After a moment, the chimes started, and it was time. Music played in the streets, and we all ran outside to each home and knocked on doors and had color thrown at us. It was magical. We spent all day going from door to door, and at the end of the day, we're jumping and dancing with laughter, color thrown and thrusted everywhere. As I danced and laughed, something in the corner of my eye caught my attention, and it was her. She was grinning from ear to ear, standing there, watching us all. Then I saw her leap in the air, flowing just like the chalk moving around us all. She turned away, and then another side of her tilted forward and spoke to me.

She said, "Hello there! What is the momentum experience of pleasure happening around you?"

I said, "It's Holi, the celebration of color play. The celebration of spring, love, good over evil. I have never seen you before—who are you?"

And then she laughed, and leaped gain, and said, "We are simply Jane, and I've just been observing and learning. Who are you?" And I introduced myself, and we danced. In a moment, she was gone.

At that moment, Jane looks at Vince and says, "I'd like you to meet someone I met long ago," and Vince gives her a confused stare. That is when Mitra makes his way to their table.

"Jane, is that you?"

And she smiles and says, "It's been a long time, Mitra. Meet my Vince" and they sit and enjoy each other's company for as long as they can.

Signe Damron is the founder of Signe-ture Publishing and a writer with 25+ years of experience. She uses her 20 years of experience in various business sectors, as well as her work with Special Olympics to build connections and foster productive relationships. In 2024, she was the recipient of the Greater Columbus Arts Council Artist Award for her first published book, French Door to Foyer.

Good News
(Biscuits and Gravy)

If I looked back far enough, I could see that my mom was aiming for this grave long before I buried her in it. Sometimes, it was like she ached for it like a kind of homesickness.

She said she drank to manage stress, and what always seemed to stress her out the most was me, despite my endless efforts to emotionally support her throughout my childhood and adolescence. She also drank to keep up with my dad. Their relationship swung between fighting and fucking, with alcohol blurring the edges of their contempt.

I hadn't been to see Mom in almost two years, but found myself standing in front of her grave the night after Halloween with marigolds and incense in my hands just a few hours after my girlfriend told me she was pregnant.

I cracked a bottle of whiskey, Black Velvet, Mom's favorite brand. Not because it was any good, but because it was cheap and she could buy it in large quantities, despite her meager income. I took a long drink, winced, and recapped the bottle before sitting in the grass, crisscross applesauce, and leaned the bottle against her headstone.

"What am I doing here?" I sat there uncertain, with no clear reason for making the trip, especially so late at night and after so long. Maybe this would be my final goodbye before removing her from my life for real and becoming the parent she always should have been. Maybe I still felt the need to share the good news about what was happening in my life since that's the only time she ever wanted to talk. It was never about what I needed or how I felt, or how she might help me. It was instead about her feeling like a good parent by hearing good news from her child. Struggles and hardships made her feel like a failure, and I trained myself to keep those things inside.

The night was silent, except for the insects chirping and trilling from the shadows. It was late, and the moon was partially cloud covered.

I assumed I was there alone. Who else but the dead would be around? As soon as the thought passed through my mind, a voice cut through the silence.

"She's kind of a bitch."

It was an older woman in an elegant but dingy dress, her hair sculpted by Aqua Net. She coughed, and a group of flies buzzed from her mouth and into the night sky.

"Who?" I croaked; it was all my throat would allow. She looked like an extra from *Beetlejuice*, with pale skin, smoky eyes, and cobwebs under one earlobe.

The woman nodded at Mom's headstone.

"You knew her?" I asked, hoping I was talking to an old friend and not a dead stranger.

"No"—the woman said—"but I know her now."

"Now?" I asked, hope evaporating. My blood rushed throughout my body.

She nodded and smiled thinly. "Want to see her? Tell her that good news of yours?"

"How did you…?" I started but stopped myself as the remaining moisture in my mouth dried up.

"Might want to take another drink before I show you," she said and winked.

Maybe it was the ease of her expression…or the fact that she reminded me of my granny, but her gaze soothed me. Lulled me into a half slumber that caused the rolling hills of the cemetery to vibrate and bounce. Pink mist seeped from the ground and wrapped itself around me like a curious octopus.

I looked at the woman for reassurance. Her eyes reflected the moon and were all I saw through the mist and shimmering stars coming into view.

"You ready?" she asked but did not wait for a response before grabbing my hand. As soon as she did, the mist pulled me to another place, but her grip kept me grounded, and I pulsed with the idea that I was safe with her there, wherever there was.

We sat on hills similar to those at the cemetery, only in that they were hills. The tendrils of grass glistened white, soft like the fur of a kitten. It cooed and sighed when I ran my hands over its surface gently.

The woman, who I decided to refer to as Granny then, sat beside me. No longer in her burial gown, she wore light capris and a loose-fitting vibrant orange shirt partially covered by an apron with daffodils on the front.

"Your mom's not around right now, but there's my John," she said, arms resting on her knees, nodding toward the sound of a waterfall I hadn't registered until then.

The falls poured a deep, murky red that collected into a pool below. I didn't allow my eyes to linger on the chunks in the pool long enough to identify what they were. Bits of cloth and hair lapped at the edges of the kitten-fur grass.

Waist deep in what I chose to think of as water was a man in denim overalls. He wore a white T-shirt underneath, the collar worn away in bits. He was mostly bald, with long strands of hair jutting off in several directions. His eyes, the parts that should have been white, were the color of the water, red and pulsing and frenzied. He looked at the pool as if it were air and he was suffocating, then dunked his head under.

"He'll be out soon," Granny said, her soothing voice tugging me away from the momentary horrors. She had a streak of flour on her cheek and she kneaded dough on a countertop that had materialized from nowhere. "Your mom, on the other hand…" she continued and shrugged. "She could be under a while, and isn't the best dinner guest anyway."

I thought of Mother's Day margaritas and Christmas cognac and every other day and holiday that required no alliteration for her to drink and be hateful. I thought of all the criticisms, rejections, and bruises that I covered with long sleeves on scorching days. Not the best dinner guest was one way to put it.

"Recipes with love are a real thing, you know?" she said. "When I'm cooking, I want my food to ground people in that moment. Take them away from whatever is bothering them because you never really know when someone is just trying to not fall apart."

At that moment, John surged from the water, gasping with delight. He locked eyes on me, then shifted his gaze to Granny. His eyes widened with alarm, and he started running through the water as if nothing was impeding his progress at all. His eyes stayed locked on mine as he sprinted through the water, splashes and droplets of red surrounding his focused face. The empty rage and jealousy were unmistakable.

"Sometimes"—Granny continued, instantly soothing my anxiety and refocusing my attention—"a good biscuit and gravy are all you need to bring someone back from a dark place, if only for a little while. When I cook, I imagine my food healing them. I imagine it lifting their spirits and bringing their hearts closer to mine." She said this while kneading and folding, kneading and folding.

"You don't want to knead too much and not for too long, otherwise the butter will start to melt, and your biscuits won't be nearly as flaky."

I nodded, unsure how to respond to the dead stranger trying to teach me how to make biscuits in the netherworld.

"You cook?" she asked.

"Yes, ma'am. Every day."

"Your mom teach you?"

A jet of air escaped from my nose, and I shook my head. "No." After a long pause, I added. "I can remember spending some time with her in the kitchen when I was young, but once her drinking got heavy, which was very early on, that all stopped."

She nodded and cut the dough into circles with a glass dusted with flour and set the rounds on a cookie sheet, ready for an oven that misted into existence in a slowly forming kitchen at the edge of nowhere.

She slid the pan of biscuits into the oven and stirred crackling bits of sausage on the stovetop before turning the dial on her Minute Minder timer.

John was nearing the edge of the kitten-fur grass and had slowed his pace. He was no longer staring at me with hateful intentions, but looking at Granny with the same kind of longing he looked at the pool with. Like she was air.

"Why are you here?" I asked Granny. "What is this place?"

For a while, she didn't respond or even acknowledge I'd spoken. She was stirring milk into the flour-dusted sausage at that point, focused on her objective.

"After the war, he was just different. All my girlfriends said the same about their husbands and boyfriends. They just went through so much, you know?"

She looked at me with a desperation in her gaze that instantly broke me. "Of course," I said, wondering which war she was referring to.

"He'd drink all the time with his Army buddies, but his real drinking was done at home." She stirred the gravy more and more aggressively as she spoke. "I became an expert with concealers," she said, and smiled at me as if looking for approval.

I nodded, trying not to suffocate on what she was saying because it was clear she knew the same kind of destructive chaos I was familiar with.

"There was this one day the kids were at school and

John was...in a way...and just certain I was doing something I shouldn't have been doing with the neighbor down the road," she said, steaming bits of gravy that splashed up on her face as she stirred. "And he shot a hole in the kitchen wall behind me. Had to go get a China cabinet that afternoon to place in front of the hole so the kids wouldn't see. That cabinet stayed in that spot for thirty years," she said. "Empty. No China. Just an empty cabinet covering a shotgun blast."

I didn't know what to say. There wasn't really anything to say other than I'm sorry, so I did, and then placed my hand over hers.

Eventually, she shrugged and pulled her hand back. "But anyway, this is where I'm supposed to be," she said. "It's what I promised him, and besides, just look at him now," she said. Her head tilted with delight as she watched him stroll up to the counter.

John's overalls and eaten-away undershirt were replaced by a suit. His hair now full and slicked back. Eyes bright and focused on her. A small smile fixed at the corner of his mouth.

She slid a plate in front of him, and he sat down at a newly formed counter, gasped with delight at the steaming plate of love in front of him, then reached across the counter to caress her suddenly younger cheek.

"What about my mom?" I asked. "Am I going to see her, or did you just bring me here to teach me how to make biscuits?"

Granny smiled, despite my sarcasm, as my mom slowly surfaced. Granny nodded in her direction and went about cleaning flour off the countertops.

Mom emerged from the water dramatically, as she always used to do everything. Making an entrance was much more important to her than anything else she did after.

She had kelp for hair, and it hung in slimy strands around her face. Her skin had taken on the color of the water, making her features hard to distinguish, except for her eyes. They locked onto mine, unblinking.

There seemed to be a moment of clarity or recognition, but then her brow furrowed slightly, and she took a couple of lurching steps backward before submerging again.

"So"—Granny said, letting the word hang in the air for a moment—"why are you here tonight? Just to pass along the mysterious good news?"

"Did I say something out loud, or did you just know what I was thinking? Because I'm pretty sure I didn't say a word."

She smiled and explained matter-of-factly that she could hear thoughts when they were attached to something painful. "The worse the pain, the more clearly I can understand the thoughts. I got the gist but couldn't get past *good news*."

I nodded and was ready to let a hundred questions spill out of my mouth about the concept she'd just explained, but the likelihood that any of this was really happening was minimal. So, I said nothing in response.

"It *is* happening," she said.

"Cute," I responded. "Anyway, the good news is that my girlfriend is pregnant. I'm going to be a dad."

The smile that took over her face lit up the fading kitchen, and not metaphorically. She beamed at me and clutched one hand to her chest. Under other circumstances, it would have been unsettling, but in the same way she could hear thoughts associated with pain, I suddenly heard thoughts associated with joy. And her thoughts saturated every molecule of my body.

"Congratulations," she finally said.

I thanked her. Then her eyes flicked over my shoulder, back toward the water, and some of her light faded. I turned, and Mom was re-emerging.

The kelp was gone, replaced by the thick jet-black hair I'd known my whole life. Her complexion had cleared of the red, and her eyes, a vibrant chestnut, locked onto mine.

I couldn't hear any of Mom's thoughts, but Granny's celebratory expressions still tumbled throughout my mind.

I never saw him leave, but John's plate of biscuits and gravy was scraped clean and sitting beside me. Looking around

Mom, as she continued her approach, I saw John's once again mostly bald head sink under the surface. Granny's thoughts faltered and then went silent as soon as he went under.

Mom looked better than I remembered seeing her in life. Her hair shone and tumbled gracefully over her shoulders. Her skin was clear and free of the typical signs of alcoholism I'd grown accustomed to. She smiled, exposing perfect porcelain teeth.

"Hey, Mom," I said.

"What's she so happy about?" Mom asked. Her cheek twitched as she nodded in Granny's direction.

A familiar sensation emerged in the center of my chest. A tightness and tugging. My heart rate increased, and my temple pulsed.

"Uh, well, Mom. I have some good news."

Her head tilted with anticipation, the porcelain smile frozen in place, but she said nothing.

"I'm going to be a father," I said. "My girlfriend is pregnant. Just told me tonight, and I came here to tell you."

"But you told her first?"

The tightness in my chest turned into a black hole of pressure. At first, I said nothing in response.

"Is that all you have to say?" I asked.

She scoffed and rolled her eyes, the porcelain now hidden between tight lips. "Well, obviously, congratulations," she said. She sighed and looked at her feet, then looked back to me pleadingly. "But why did you tell her first? She's no one."

"She was here, and she asked."

Mom opened her mouth to respond, but I cut her off and added, "Besides, you were busy." That comment floated over a long silence.

"It's not like I knew you were coming," she said.

"Yeah," I said. "That's a response."

She held out her hands with a *what do you want from me* kind of expression that I was so familiar with.

"Anyway, I wanted to tell you the good news, and I have.

Now I want to go back," I said and turned back toward Granny. The kitchen had vanished and was replaced by stars and an inky black night sky. "Can you take me back now, please?"

"Wait," Mom said, and when I turned back to ask why, her appearance was drastically different. There were splotches of red all over her face. The vibrant chestnut had dulled. Her skin sagged, and half her hair had turned back to kelp that dripped slime on her shoulders.

"Do you hate me?" she asked.

"No, Mom, I don't hate you."

I hated her more than anyone I'd ever known. I hated her with an intensity that frightened me at times, but I also loved her with the same kind of intensity and could never tell her how I felt because she'd never truly listen. Simple answers and statements that were affirming and positive were all that ever seemed to take hold.

"Yes, you do," she hissed and turned, lurching back toward the water, mumbling aggressively under her breath.

"Here," Granny said, and slid her recipe book across the counter toward me, breaking the focus on my mother. "Let's get you home."

When I picked up the book, I couldn't make out any of the words, and it started to slowly melt in my hands. I looked toward Granny but couldn't find her shape. It was too soft and wavered in and out of sight. The moonlight was returning and shining through her.

I closed my eyes and smelled butter and sausage, then heard the sound of my mom calling my name from the kitchen in my childhood home and felt my little fingers tying the canvas straps on her apron. It was when things were still good.

Her vibrant chestnut eyes held mine as she gently cupped my cheek in one hand while using the other to dust flour from my cheek.

When I opened my eyes, I was alone again in the moonlit cemetery with a bottle and her tombstone.

While I was in that other place with Granny, the bottle

got uncapped and tipped over. It lay in the grass, empty. Beneath it was a recipe card with daffodils around the perimeter, just like on Granny's apron. The recipe for biscuits and gravy was written in shaky but elegant cursive. The "from" line didn't have a name, just a heart drawn in red.

BISCUITS AND SAUSAGE GRAVY

2 cups flour
4 tsp baking powder
1 tbsp sugar
¾ tsp salt
1 cup milk
1 stick butter (put in freezer at beginning of prep)

Combine all dry ingredients and thoroughly mix. Using pastry cutter, cut in butter until dough has coarse crumbles. Add milk and mix well, but don't overmix. Knead on a floured surface 6-8 times and fold in half. Roll out dough and fold again. Repeat this process 2-3 times and finally roll to approx. 1 inch thickness. Handle the dough as little as possible during kneading to keep the butter cold. Cut into circles with flour-dusted glass. Bake at 425 (convection) or 450 for 10-12 minutes on an ungreased cookie sheet.

1 pound breakfast sausage
2 cups milk
1 cup half-n-half
3 tbsp flour
2 tbsp butter
1 tsp pepper
½ tsp salt
¼ tsp red pepper flakes

Cook sausage in a skillet. Add flour and stir to coat sausage. Cook 1-2 minutes while stirring. Slowly add milk and half-and-half, stirring regularly. Slowly bring to a simmer and allow to thicken. Add butter and seasoning, mix and serve.

Confession
(Chocolate Chip Cookies)

It was Father's Day, the hardest day of the year for my mom since my dad passed away. He had seemed to have a stranglehold on his cancer, but then funding got cut at the VA, his doctor ended up in the private sector, and Dad was dead a month later. The last two years had been the same— my brother and I distracting Mom for a couple of days before extracting ourselves back to our own lives.

But I was only there physically. The rest of me was wholly consumed by a chaotic ocean of thoughts, my vision focused on the quarter-sized dot of tile on the kitchen floor in front of me, though I wasn't really looking at the tile, but through it. What I envisioned was the desert. Ripples of heat rose off the barren landscape, and the furnace wind blasted against my cheeks. In the distance, I heard sporadic gunfire and overlapping screams until it was just the wind again, the distant voices silenced.

If my mom turned around and saw me, I'd have looked as if in a trance, or paralyzed by some waking nightmare. She pulled the pan of cookies from the oven, and the smell overpowered the poison sloshing around inside my skull.

The scent was wonderful, but the aroma did more than wake up my senses. It made me recall one of the many times when I was a kid helping my mom in the kitchen so clearly that I felt transported.

My orange apron with yellow polka dots had a pocket in front that always had a little baggie of Honey Nut Cheerios inside. One sniff of the past, and I was out of the desert and into the safest place I could remember.

The memory snapped me out of it so much I could almost hear the sound of bare feet slapping the linoleum floor of my childhood home as I crossed the kitchen to fetch eggs from the fridge. I closed my eyes and pictured that kitchen, with its pastel paisley wallpaper and my mom's gentle hands reaching down to pick me up.

A delighted squeal would escape from my insides when she hoisted me—hands under my armpits—onto the beige plastic stool she kicked around the kitchen to reach the high cabinets.

She'd let me crack the eggs into the mixing bowl, one at a time, and would celebrate my success every time I managed to avoid getting pieces of shell in the bowl. Vibrant orange globs dropped into creamed butter and sugar, her hand over mine as we stirred the contents together. Music played in the background. She always had music on when she cooked. In fact, it wasn't just when she cooked; she had a song in her heart and in her step when she did most things.

"What are you singing?" my mom asked, snapping me from the trance entirely.

"I *was* singing?" I asked.

She turned from the oven to face me, and as she did, the humored smile she wore dropped away, and morphed into motherly concern.

"You're all sweaty, hun. Are you OK? Want me to turn up the air?"

I shook my head, wiping at my brow. "I *was* singing!" I said. Not a question anymore, but a bemused exclamation. I couldn't remember the name of the song, something that no doubt entered my mind through a Walkman with orange foam earphones sometime in the '80s, if not in the kitchen with Mom, but that didn't matter. What mattered was that I was singing in the first place.

Singing in the kitchen was something I'd done my whole life, starting in that orange apron with yellow polka dots, but hadn't done so in years. Not since the depression took hold after my last deployment and an immoveable black hole spontaneously formed in the center of my chest.

For a long time, I stopped singing. Dishes lingered in the sink and on the coffee table in front of the TV. I forgot about enough bills that I had to set everything to auto-pay after threats of eviction. And I couldn't even remember the last time I'd changed the oil in my car or finished reading a book. I was sinking in place. Alive but not living.

My mother's concern was morphing into confusion that she appeared close to just accepting and dismissing, as she often would when my brother and I were both still home and we exhausted her with our strangeness. Instead, she stopped mixing the next batch and set the bowl aside on the counter.

"Are you OK?" she asked. It wasn't a passing question. I could see from her expression that it was an actual question. She *truly* wanted to know how I was.

An old urge resurfaced in an instant, like it wasn't involuntary anymore to brush off the moment and lie to her.

To say *Yes, Mama. I'm OK, just glad to be here*, and let her smile, nod, and move on, but I couldn't lie to her, or anyone else, anymore.

I'm OK. I'm fine. It was a lie that only seemed to protect others from having to deal with me, but it never made my problems any more manageable. The more I held in, the more unmanageable everything became, but I'd been swallowing pain my whole life, for whatever reason, and letting it out felt a bit like vomiting.

"Not really, Mom," I said quietly.

The instantaneous swell of concern that flooded her

expression made me falter. I never did like burdening her, but I needed more than a cookie, as healing as hers were. What I really needed was for her to truly see me and still want to place her hand on my cheek like she did when I was a little boy.

I felt tainted, and thought if I opened up to her, she'd agree, but I was poisoning myself with silence. Opening that doorway for her was horrifying at first, but was relieving in ways I couldn't put into words as soon as the horror evaporated.

I let out a long, shaky breath. "No, Mom. I'm pretty far from OK."

She let out a long breath of her own, her shoulders slumping like she was deflating. Then she straightened, her apron was off, and she was around the counter, sitting down on the stool next to mine in a flash. She rested her hands on mine.

They were always so warm, probably because she seemed to never stop using them.

"What's going on?" she asked in her gentle Southern drawl. Every time she was in the kitchen, that Mississippi farm girl accent came creeping back.

I'd finally told the truth for once—*I'm not OK*—and she was there and seemed receptive, but I didn't even know where to begin. I couldn't manage the torrent of poisonous thoughts in my mind, so I had difficulty figuring a way to get them out of my mouth in an order that made sense instead of flooding her with years of emotional trauma she couldn't decipher.

"It's OK, baby. Just one thing at a time," she said, obviously sensing the chaotic uncertainty inside me.

"I just feel like if I tell you some of this stuff, you won't see me the same way. That you'll want to move your hands off mine," I said.

She immediately squeezed both hands and didn't let up. "Never," she said.

I didn't need to tell her everything, and not for the first time, I realized a therapist might be a good idea. For now, what I needed to tell my mom was the one thing I'd never tell a therapist or anyone else, because it'd likely land me in prison.

Though I wouldn't say what I did was the "right thing" to do, it certainly didn't feel wrong. I just needed someone else to agree, and then maybe I'd be able to let it go and move forward with my life.

"It was my third deployment, and I'd made the decision long before getting those orders that I wouldn't re-enlist," I said, then took a sip of water and wiped my sweaty palms on my pants. She grabbed my hands back when I was done and continued squeezing.

"I didn't know what I was going to do on the outside and had no plan other than to get out. There wasn't much combat that last deployment. Our mission was primarily training and protection, yet I'd never seen so much death and destruction." I paused.

"The worst part of it for me was the kids."

Her grip tightened on my hands. "Oh, God," she whispered hoarsely.

"Right from the beginning of the deployment, I started finding kids dead in the streets, most of them from age three to maybe eight. Many of the kids had what I could only assume was their parent, usually the mom, dead beside them."

She slowly pulled one hand away and placed it on her mouth, letting out a long sigh.

"At first, it was just an awful thing to see in an ocean of awful things, you know?" I said, and she nodded, dislodging a tear that zigzagged down her cheek to her trembling hand.

"But after the third or fourth kid, I started looking more closely, and every single one of the kids I found, their parents, too, were killed with expert shots. Heart and head almost every time."

Mom made a guttural sound laced with disgust, sorrow, and terrible understanding.

"We'd go into a neighborhood providing protection, while the local army gathered intelligence from the community. Every time we were on maneuvers, another child, another family, another pile." I didn't realize my foot was nervously bouncing off the floor until my mom gently placed her hand on my leg to still me. The look of sorrow in her eyes hurt in a way I couldn't articulate.

More tears zigzagged down her cheek, and for a moment, so much of me wanted to stop. To go back in time and tell her *I'm* OK. This was a heavy burden to place on such a beautiful soul, but she seemed to sense my hesitation and prodded me forward.

"There were plenty of opinions throughout the unit about who was responsible, but no one was of the opinion it was one of ours. It never even crossed my mind that it could have been one of ours."

I let out a long sigh. Mom wiped her tears away and suddenly looked more angry than sad, like she knew what I was going to say next.

"Couple more trips outside the fence. Couple more dead kids. The next time out, there was some commotion with one local, and as soon as I went around the corner of this blasted-out building, I saw this little girl, maybe four or five, standing on the sidewalk fifty yards away from me. And my heart just sank," I said and paused. I could see her so clearly on that street. The black hole in my chest flared, and I could practically feel my blood rushing throughout my body. My mom took a shaky breath.

"Someone called to the little girl. She turned around, and the back of her head exploded."

My mom said nothing. What was there to say? Horror washed over her features as a weighty silence pressed on us both. When the tightness in my chest subsided a little, I continued.

"The woman who called to the little girl screamed after she was shot and ran over to her. I think I called out to her. I think I told her to get down. To look out. Something," I said, looking desperately at my mom, needing her to know I tried. "But if she heard me, she gave no indication, and she was shot seconds later. Everyone else was busy detaining some of the locals being questioned, and I saw where the shot came from.

"I went into the building and made my way up to the fourth floor, and right before I went into the room the shot came from, a sergeant from one of our companion units came walking out."

"And what happened?" Mom asked.

"At first, I couldn't really say anything. I was just stunned that it was one of our guys and not some evil militant sniper on the loose that I could have taken care of. Then the rage took over, and I started questioning him. I told him about the two who were just shot and said it looked like the shot came from where he was. He brushed it off at first, then got defensive and pulled rank. Told me I was crazy and to keep my crazy bullshit to myself."

"Did you?"

"Absolutely not," I said. "I went to the commander and reported him the next day after getting back to base." I took another drink of water and looked outside after something sped past the window. There was another blur of movement outside, and then I saw it, the hummingbird that loved to come into my mother's garden for nectar.

"But"—I continued, refocusing my attention on Mom— "the commander not only didn't want to hear it, they were furious with me for daring to suggest something so monstrous, and told me if I spoke another word about it I'd be looking at time in Fort Leavenworth before I was dishonorably discharged."

"Unbelievable."

I sat with the memories of the anger and confusion I'd felt. It wasn't just the personal threats and the individual actions; it put everything into question for me. "And he put me on additional details. The shit jobs only given to those under disciplinary actions."

"So nothing happened to this guy?"

I sighed and went quiet for a long moment. "At first," I said.

"OK…what does that mean?"

I stared at the floor, saying nothing while she gently

stroked my hand with one thumb. The grandfather clock in the other room was the only sound in the house.

"Command wouldn't do anything about it. I told some of the other guys in the unit, and they thought I was crazy too. Most of the guys stopped talking to me altogether, so I just dropped it and let a little time pass.

"Our units went outside the fence together many times. I was familiar with his movements and the types of locations he liked to set up, and I'd been looking at his horrific crime scenes for months and felt like I could anticipate him and hopefully take advantage of an opportunity, if one presented itself."

"Opportunity?" Mom asked.

"I saw him go into a building to set up and followed him. Gave him time to get set up and get comfortable while I pinned down his exact location. I heard him move around on the floor above me and went up."

The rest of the house was silent, except for the gentle *tick-tock* from the other room. Mom even seemed to hold her breath. I took a drink of water, starting to speak, but couldn't quite get the words to come out. So I took another drink and swiped a hand across my damp forehead. Mom caressed the back of my palm with her thumb. I took a deep breath, let it out slowly, and then told her the rest.

"I had a sidearm no one knew about. Confiscated it off an enemy combatant pretty early on. Most of the guys had extra weapons of some kind. They'd frequently inventory any issued ammo back at base, so there were times you had to explain fired rounds and..." I paused and cleared my throat. "Well...I didn't want to have to explain any fired rounds." I stopped, wiped my free hand on my thigh, and barreled through the rest.

"He heard me coming and turned. At first, I lowered the gun when we made eye contact, and he lowered his. He was smirking at me nervously, and then got mad when I didn't say anything.

"He said, 'What the fuck are you doing in here? Still on this thing about me shooting kids? You think you're better than me? Who cares anyway if I shoot some of these filthy little...' and that's as far as he got before I raised my weapon and shot him."

Mom sat in stunned silence.

"I removed all his identifying markers and buried his body under the surrounding rubble in the room where he was lying in wait. Went back to my unit and finished out the day. Never said another word about him to anyone. I heard from a friend of someone in his unit that he was listed as MIA. Last I checked, he still was."

When the last of it was out of my mouth, I could barely breathe. My heart rate was erratic. There was a massive weight on my chest, and my hearing was so muffled by dread and the pounding of my heart that it almost felt like I was under water.

My mom put her hands back on mine and gave them a gentle squeeze. "Um," she said and paused for a long time. It was only five or ten seconds, but I'd never endured longer ticks on the clock. "You obviously have good reason to be troubled by the things you've seen and done, but I hope killing that man is not one of them," she said.

Now I sat in stunned silence as my heart rate normalized.

"You said you were afraid I'd look at you differently if you told me these things, and I said I wouldn't. But that actually isn't true. I have always been awed by you and your kindness toward others. You joined the Army to make a difference, and however naive that might have been,"—she said, with a look I remembered well from when I'd enlisted and she was expressing her dissent—"you were sent places you never should have been sent by corrupt people upholding corrupt institutions and policies. And when you tried to report literal war crimes, you were punished and called insane."

She placed her hands on my cheeks and gave me the look I loved from the moment I first saw it when I was little. The look that said *everything will be fine, and I love you like no other.*

"Fuck all that and fuck that guy. He deserved it. Let me get you a cookie," she said, patted my hands, and stood up. The weight on my chest vanished.

"I thought if anyone took this news well, it'd be you," I said. "But I wasn't really expecting this level of understanding."

She laughed, just a little short burst of air through the nose. "Don't get me wrong, I'm not trying to condone violence, and I'm definitely not encouraging you to seek out more *opportunities*. I love the show *Dexter*, but I don't want you to *be* Dexter. But the way I see it, you had two choices. Let him keep murdering children and their family members who came to grieve over them, or stop him. You did what you had to do, and I'm proud of you," she said, and set a glass of milk and a plate with two cookies in front of me.

"Thanks, Mom," I said, and after a moment's hesitation added, "Do you think Dad would have understood?"

She straightened herself and put her hands on her hips, looking at me with a hint of agitated disappointment, like I was ten years old again and had just broken her favorite vase.

"Of course. He was an Army man through and through, but he was a good man with a good heart first. He would have understood. I think he would have done the same thing if put in the same position. You cannot stand idly by while atrocities are committed. He absolutely would have understood."

"Thanks, Mom. And Happy Father's Day on his behalf."

"Thank you for being with me today. It's always difficult, and having you boys around makes it easier."

As if on cue, the doorbell rang. And rang again. And rang five more times. My little brother was home.

CHOCOLATE CHIP COOKIES

2 sticks (one cup) butter
1 ½ cups sugar
2 TBSP molasses
1 tsp vanilla
2 eggs
2 ¼ cups flour
1 tsp baking soda
1 tsp salt
2 TBSP honey
1/3 cup peanut butter
1 bag semisweet chocolate chips

INSTRUCTIONS

Soften/melt butter. Add sugar, molasses, and vanilla. Mix well. Add eggs. Mix well.

Add flour, baking soda, and salt. Mix well. Add honey and peanut butter. Mix well. Fold in chocolate chips. Dough will be sticky, so it's best to use a scooper. Bake at 350 (convection) or 375 for approximately 10 minutes.

Family Flavor
(Peanut Clusters)

Dad wouldn't stop calling. He'd been talking about some ancient family traditional holiday for close to a year, making sure I knew to attend the festivities he'd planned. I'd told him at least a dozen times I'd be there, despite secretly trying to formulate a good reason not to attend.

As the date approached, the volume of his texts and phone calls seeking reassurance and confirmation reached the point where I was genuinely uncomfortable about the whole ordeal. Something seemed off. Dad sounded different, and Mom was as quiet about it as he was vocal.

Mom was *always* trying to get me to come back home to visit, but not for the strange holiday my father was so excited about. She'd said nothing about that, and even seemed uncomfortable about it herself, offering only vague information about what would take place and why. Something about salt harvesting and a ceremony on the beach.

According to my father, it was an ancient tradition to honor the ocean that had provided so much for our ancestors throughout their lives. He said it was an important holiday to our ancestors, but he'd never talked about it until last year. Granted, the ocean meant a great deal to our family and was the source of my parents' wealth. My father ran a small but lucrative salt company. They harvested locally, and restaurants around the world, especially high-end ones, used it obsessively.

I expressed no interest in the family business, but Dad made sure I knew from an early age he didn't want me to be involved and to find my own path because he had plans to hand the company down to my younger brother.

Despite my unease and general confusion about the never mentioned but, apparently, long-standing family tradition, I was looking forward to lying on the beach under the low hanging cliffs near our family home and listening to the waves more than anything. I loved the city and couldn't imagine living anywhere else, but I often ached for the ocean with a kind of homesickness that should be reserved for my family and home.

My phone buzzed. It was a text from Dad.
What time are you getting to the airport?
9:30
You sure that's early enough for an 11:30 flight?
Should be fine
Chicago is busy though…

I sighed. I'd flown out of Chicago a dozen times, and yes, it's busy. But every time, I showed up two hours early. And every time, I sat in the terminal waiting for half an hour for my flight to board while reading one of many romantasy novels my boyfriend referred to as elf porn, though not as a criticism. He read the genre as much as I did.

Dad started typing again, the three little text bubbles dancing on my screen, so I rushed to beat him to it.
I'll get there at 8:30, Dad. Just in case…

I would not be getting there at 8:30, but had no interest in debating it with him.

The bubbles vanished and then resurfaced. *Probably for the best. Where are you parking?*

"Oh, for fuck's sake," I said, then filled a small glass with orange juice and put a piece of bread in the toaster.

Gotta run. Hopping in the shower. Can't wait to see you!
Neither thing was true. Sometimes, I just had to cut off conversations with him unless I wanted every thought, feeling, intention, and action questioned and second-guessed, even at forty. I drank the last of my juice and liberally applied honey butter to my toast.

It wasn't that I didn't want to see my family. I was looking forward to it and actually needed some time away from the city after being downsized from my social work position at Veteran's Affairs. Three months of severance for a fifteen-year career. I had no disciplinary issues and was even awarded Social Worker of the Quarter the week before they let me go along with many others.

I already had another job in the works, but I needed the beach. The ocean air and sunshine with zero traffic noise bearing down on me. That and my mom's cooking. Specifically, her peanut clusters.

I'd eat anything and everything she put on a plate in front of me, but her peanut clusters were my favorite indulgence. It was something we always made together every time I visited home. The special touch was the locally harvested salt flakes from the family company that she sprinkled on top.

My stomach rumbled loud enough to startle me, and I had to laugh at myself after shushing it. My phone buzzed again.

Text when you get through security?
He had never been so concerned about any visit in the past. Never asked me a hundred times to come visit, that was always left up to Mom. Never asked me to text him when I made it through security. Never even kept tabs on me when I was a teenager. That was always mom. It was strange, but he was also getting older. Maybe he just kept forgetting he'd already asked me to come home.

It'll be fine, dad…I'll text you when I land.
The three dots appeared and danced on my screen for a long time. Then they went away, and there was a long pause.

The dots returned. *OK, sweetie. See you in a few hours.*

Landed, I texted Dad when the pilot said we were free to use our devices again.

Your brother is picking you up. I'll let him know.

With all his efforts to ensure I came to the new/old family holiday, I was surprised he wasn't the one to pick me up. I figured he'd be dying to see me, but whatever.

The car ride home felt off in the same way Dad's behavior did. My relationship with my brother, Paul, had always been more surface level, but we were still brother and sister. Things were never awkward between us, but the ride home was strange. Paul seemed distracted. At first, he put the radio on so loud we couldn't talk, and when I finally convinced him to turn it down, he was slow to respond to my questions. Any time our eyes met, he immediately averted his. Maybe it was just issues with the business, which was the only thing he talked about for more than two seconds.

"Things will be better when we fix our supply issues and the stock price rebounds," he said.

"Supply issues?" I asked. "I didn't realize you could ever run out of sea salt… I mean, the ocean covers most of the planet. What kind of supply issues?"

He sighed and shook his head. It was the same kind of expression as when our father was disappointed with a bad report card. "Our salt is special. It's unique. We can't just get it from anywhere."

"So what are you going to do?" I asked.

"Dad has a plan. I'm helping. We'll work it out," he said and looked over at me with a reassuring smile that didn't touch his eyes. "Reviving this holiday and doing the little ceremony on the beach is kind of the start of that."

"Hmm," I said. "Well, yeah. I mean…yeah, I hope it helps or works or…yeah." I picked at my cuticles as I stammered through my halting response. What Paul was saying made no sense. How would an old ancestral holiday and a little ceremony on the beach help their supply or stock price? For a second, I wanted to ask him if he thought Dad still had all his mental faculties and if he should consider taking over the business sooner than planned. But I stared out the window instead, saying nothing.

Paul turned into the driveway, a long winding road leading up to the house, where Mom and Dad stood on the wrap-around porch, waving. Adirondack chairs were set on one side of the porch. An outdoor sofa and grill on the other. A mound of firewood piled up in one corner.

We got out, said hello, and grabbed my luggage before Mom whisked me away to the kitchen to help her prepare the peanut clusters.

"Are you OK, Mom?" I asked.

"What do you mean?"

I shrugged and hesitated. "Your eyes are just kind of baggy. I didn't want to say anything out there, but it looks like you've been crying."

"No," Mom said, waving at me dismissively, but she turned away. "Just tired, sweetie. Haven't slept much the last few nights."

"Any idea why?"

She wiped at the counter, though it was clean. "Not all that unusual," she said. "I'll be fine. Can you get out the double boiler?"

I did as she requested and then added an inch or so of water to the bottom pot, topped it, and turned on the heat. "Chips still in the pantry, or do you have them out already?"

"Right here," Mom said, sliding over a bag of milk chocolate chips that were hiding under a tea cloth.

A gentle breeze slipped through the house from the open windows. The smell of the ocean was overwhelming in the best way. Gulls circled in the sky, cawing at the fish below. There were no trains, no cars, no gunshots or angry shouts like I'd grown accustomed to in Chicago. Just wind, mildly crashing waves, and the soft, meandering whistle that always escaped my mom's mouth when she was busy in the kitchen.

After melting the chocolate, mixing in the peanuts, and spooning them onto a cookie sheet to cool, I plopped down into a chair at the dinette table in the corner of the kitchen.

"Let me get you some lunch," Mom said. "I made tuna salad just for you."

"The one with apples?" I asked hopefully.

"The same."

"Yes!"

"I'll get you some iced tea too."

"Thanks, Mom."

She plated the tuna and set it in front of me, then went to fill a glass with tea. When she turned around with the full glass, she was stirring it, and she set the spoon on the counter when she saw me looking at her.

"What are you stirring into my tea, lady? Slipping me a Mickey?" I asked and laughed with my mouth still full of food.

Mom flushed a little. "Just some lemon."

"Mom," I groaned. "You know I don't like that."

"Just a little," she said apologetically. "It balances out the flavor."

"Fine," I said, not really irritated, and took the drink from her. I couldn't taste the lemon at all, so I thought she did use just a little. And iced tea in the kitchen with Mom was as much of a staple as the tuna salad and peanut clusters.

"You should head down to the beach after you eat," Mom said. "It's a really beautiful day, and I have some preparations to make anyway."

"Great idea," I said, ready to finish up and get down there. I'd been aching for the beach for a while.

Despite Dad's eagerness to get me home, I'd only seen him for the first few minutes when I arrived. He'd disappeared as soon as Mom had scooped me up into the kitchen. In fact, my brother must have disappeared with him because I hadn't seen him either. I guessed they were just letting me and Mom catch up.

I slathered on sunscreen, put on my two-piece, and slipped on a sundress over that. It was my favorite sleeveless fire engine red short dress that traveled with me everywhere, the red fading after years of time in the sun.

Mom saw me out the door, scolding me for passing on her suggestion that I take a sun cap. I went out the back door and down the steps at the far end of the yard that had beach access.

It'd been too long since I'd been on this beach, and I instantly felt at home as soon as my feet touched the sand. There were only a few people on the beach, all of them in the far distance. A couple of boats were tiny specks on the horizon. The beach was mine.

I slid off my sundress and laid on the sand, an instantaneous and almost euphoric calm washing over me. It was warm but not sweltering, the sun above me inviting. There was a gentle breeze coming off the water, and the only clouds in the sky were picturesque in the distance above the water. The peace and beauty of the afternoon washed over me, and feeling at peace for the first time in ages, I closed my eyes and drifted off to sleep, the lapping of the ocean waves lulling me.

An hour or so later, based on the position of the sun, I woke up, my skin tingling. The tide had come in and was washing over me, but not high enough to go over my mouth or nose. The warm water seemed to cling to me, like a creature seeking reassurance.

I felt a little strange, my head swimming a bit. *Probably just from sleep.* As I moved my head from side to side, the sky and clouds above me blurred and skipped through the sky in my vision. I tried to sit up, but could only raise my head a little.

There was an intensifying tingling going up my hands and arms, and when I looked down at them, little pieces of flesh, like grains of sand, separated from me and dissolved into the water. I tried to sit up but couldn't, and forced my left hand over to the right side to rub at the dissolving section of my forearm. The skin was soft, thinning, and sliding away into the surf.

I panicked, an immense weight suddenly in the center of my chest, but I could barely move. When I tried to stand, my legs sank into the sand as the tide rose.

Water lapped over my face, and I coughed and gagged, nostrils burning. *Why can't I move?* It was a panicked question that raced through my mind a thousand times in an instant.

I called out for help, but there was no one else on the empty beach. With great effort, I lifted my head to see the last ship blink out of existence at the edge of the horizon.

I laid my head back down in the sand, warm water rippling around my ears, and felt a momentary calm, like this was supposed to be happening.

More of my body broke away and dissolved into the ocean. The knot on my bathing suit top dissolved, and the water caused the top to slip out of position enough to expose a nipple. I was about to cry out for help again when a figure appeared on the edge of the low cliffs above me. After a minute, my eyes adjusted, and I saw it was my father, looking down at me on the beach below.

"Daddy!" I cried out, but he didn't move or speak. "Daddy! Help me!"

The water no longer felt like water but hands, strong hands, gripping me everywhere. Pulling me deeper into the sand. Pulling me deeper into the water.

My brother slowly walked up on the left side of my father, soon followed by my mother on his right side.

More of my body dissolved into the ocean. The water hands gripped tighter, pulled harder.

More people showed up on the cliffs beside my family until there were at least fifty people watching me dissolve from above. My father raised his hands up to the sky as if in praise and shouted words indistinguishable to me. His gaze shifted from the sky to me, and he dropped to his knees, hands outstretched toward me.

I reached for him, but enough of my elbow had dissolved that my arm broke off and slipped down my side, caressing my vanishing thigh until invisible hands swept it up and dragged it underneath. The little air bubbles popping at the surface were the only evidence of my arm's prior existence.

In my final moments, I felt the currents, the depths, the ancient life within the ocean, and for a moment, understood what my family had done. I was truly a part of things now.

PEANUT CLUSTERS

One twelve-ounce bag of milk chocolate chips (NOT semisweet)
12 ounces salted peanuts
½ tsp salt
Sea salt flakes

INSTRUCTIONS

Melt milk chocolate chips in a double boiler (or microwave), stirring until smooth. Add ½ tsp salt and peanuts. Mix until well coated. Scoop teaspoons of mix onto parchment paper covered cookie sheet and tap down a little to flatten. Allow to cool for 15 minutes before sprinkling with sea salt flakes (preferably locally harvested from a family company). Let cool on the counter for at least another 45 minutes before moving to the refrigerator to solidify. Ready to eat in 2 hours. Best served cold. Store in an airtight container in the refrigerator.

Duncan's Heart
(Granola)

My parents had two visitors for the week: one broken son and a 180-pound Great Dane named Duncan, who they were watching for my older brother while he went to Mexico with his wife and daughters.

Duncan looked closer to a cow than a dog, not only because of his size but his short white fur with black splotches, his muzzle and belly a pale pink. He clomped through the house and awkwardly galloped through the yard on summer days.

He had Addison's disease, and when my brother and sister-in-law first rescued him, he was frail and much lighter, with no appetite and severe depression. After a few months of being smothered with love and patience, he was transformed, the symptoms of his disease going almost entirely into remission. His vet would have normally chastised the pet parent for having an overweight dog, but she said that an overweight dog with Addison's was simply unheard of and to keep doing what they were doing.

I'd only spent a little time with Duncan over the years because our family is scattered throughout the country, but I cherished the time I got to spend with him.

I was visiting for my parents' fifty-third anniversary. Not a banner year like twenty-five or fifty, so there wasn't a big celebration, just me and Duncan and some wonderful home-cooked food, some of which I smelled wafting under the bedroom door, my mother's granola.

Their anniversary weekend coincided with Passover. For reasons that never made sense to me, my parents—lifelong Southern Baptists—observed the holiday. As an atheist, it made less sense for me to participate, but I was there. And it was always amusing to watch my dad choke down the traditional Seder meal that I enjoyed, despite my lack of connection to the tradition.

The combined holiday weekend also coincided with the finalization of my divorce from the woman I'd been married to for over eight years. Not an anticipated development in my life, to say the least. Celebrating marriage wasn't exactly at the top of my list at that moment, but I wasn't really there to celebrate my parent's wedding anniversary or Passover, despite my love of wine, Charoset, and watching my dad squirm.

I was there because of the pistol in my nightstand drawer at home. I couldn't stop looking at it. Before bed and when I got up first thing, I'd open the drawer and wonder which category of statistics I'd be placed under.

Would I write a note explaining it all, and if so, who would I address it to? If I didn't write a note, would people assume it was because of the divorce? The betrayal? The additional loss of my job, health insurance, and disability benefits all at the same time, which also caused the loss of access to the medical procedures that made my life livable? Was it because the country I'd volunteered to let ravage my mind and body had turned its back on me when I'd finished killing their enemies? Was it because of the killing? The chronic pain and nightmares? Was it because I was lonely and felt worthless and had no one telling me otherwise? Would they blame themselves or just be hurt and angry with me?

I couldn't stop thinking about that pistol, even when I wasn't sitting on the edge of my bed, staring at it longingly while it waited in the shadows of my nightstand drawer, ready.

It was early in the morning, the sun sending slotted laser beams through the gaps in the blinds, and despite being a thousand miles away from my nightstand and pistol, I was still sitting there thinking about it. The drawer to my parent's guest room nightstand was open and empty, nothing metallic and liberating hiding in the shadows.

A brief wave of homesickness washed over me, then shame and disgust, followed closely by the all-too-familiar pressure in the center of my chest. My heart thudded, and I felt my blood rushing throughout my body as little black specks, like a thousand gnats buzzing around the room, clouding my vision.

There was a loud bang on the door, causing me to almost spring off the mattress in surprise. I turned on the small black lamp on the edge of the nightstand and quietly slid the drawer closed. There was a huffing sound under the door.

Duncan was sniffing for me.

There was another loud bang on the door, either one of his massive paws or his body. He sniffed again and whined quietly.

Maybe he needed to be let outside, but I heard my mom in the kitchen, which was right next to the door Duncan used to be let out.

Another sniff, another whine, another thud.

"You leave him alone, sweet boy," Mom said to Duncan from the other side of the wall. Duncan gave a pleading whine in response, and I heard his paw clomp down on the wood floor like he was trying to say, *No, I won't leave him alone.*

"What is it, honey?" Mom asked.

Duncan let out the softest bark touched with a little rumbling growl at the end that you could tell he didn't mean and was trying to soften. Mom made this wordless sound in response, but I knew the sound well, and it meant *You better not have done that, and you better correct yourself now if you did,* so I ended their standoff and opened the door to let him in.

Mom peaked around the corner to say good morning when I opened the door, her apron already dirty from use, despite the early hour. Duncan licked her hand apologetically and pressed his muzzle into her chest.

Then he turned, walked into my room, and gently closed the door in my mom's face with his backside as she let out a surprised and joyous laugh, the melody of her happiness lifting the mood in the room instantly.

Duncan pressed his muzzle into my stomach and whined. He was strong and insistent, pushing me back until I sat on the bed again. I rubbed his head and scratched behind his ears and under his chin as he licked my face and neck, taking time to gently nibble at my earlobe.

I laughed and pushed him back a little to stop the tickling sensation from turning into hysterics, and he immediately clubbed me in the center of the chest with one of his massive paws. It was hard to think of them as paws with their size and the weight behind them. They were more like tree stumps.

I set his paw down, relieving the pressure on my chest, though I preferred that kind and insistent pressure much more than the pressure I'd been feeling in my chest moments before.

He put his paw on my chest again. And this time, when I put it back down on the ground, he jumped and put both tree stump paws on my shoulders, pinning my back on the bed, his bowling ball sized head hovering above me. A small string of drool was dangerously close to my eyebrow, and his weight was overwhelming anyway. So I wrapped my arms around him in a big bear hug (or cow hug in Duncan's case) and turned him on his side so we were lying on the bed, facing each other.

There was an aching sorrow in his eyes, and he alternated between nuzzling kisses and pawing at me with his giant stumps, like *he* was petting *me*. Comforting *me*.

He'd come to the door initially when I was thinking myself worthless and wishing for the contents of my nightstand at home instead of the one at Mom and Dad's, banging and whimpering and sniffing.

I'd heard of dogs who could sniff out cancer. Maybe Duncan could sniff out heartache. Maybe it was the inevitability he could sense. Or maybe I was just desperate to believe there was anyone or anything who actually wanted me around.

"You want to go for a walk, buddy?"

Duncan licked my hands and neck, then jumped down from the bed and shook himself off, the medallions on his collar clinking off each other.

I put on shoes and grabbed his leash off the door handle of my parent's bedroom.

"That smells amazing," I said to my mom as I walked through the kitchen. I put an arm around her shoulder and kissed her cheek.

"Taking the big fella for a walk?" she asked.

"Yes, ma'am."

"Granola will be cool enough to eat in half an hour. You want it like cereal with milk and blueberries when you get back?"

"That sounds wonderful, Momma. Thank you."

We started down the street, the desert wind warm and insistent. My family moved around a lot, and I never really felt like any of the places were truly home. But Southern Nevada was the closest, despite its desolation and that the focus of its most important and visited city was to take as much money from visitors as possible.

There was a permanence to the desert, and a stark beauty I found incomparable. But my high opinion of the area dwindled in the summer, when 120° days were common. You could look out on the road and see the waves of heat broiling up from the ground, like the whole area had become an oven. Blast furnace winds ensured you'd be picking sand from your teeth and ears for days, and plastering Chapstick on cracked lips. I was grateful to be there when the weather was more tolerable.

Duncan was as pleasant on walks as anywhere else. He never tugged on the leash or harassed passersby, often welcoming as many pets from strangers as there were strangers offering them. If another dog passed, Duncan would watch them carefully but never got aggressive, and made just as many canine friends as he did human ones on the various walks we'd taken that week.

Eventually, we came upon the old baseball field that I'd spent countless hours on while growing up, and I stood there, staring at it for a long time, Duncan patiently sitting at my side.

The memories were so vibrant, I could practically see myself running around the bases and feel the hot wind against my cheeks as I dove into third base, wrapping my arms around the bag. The umpire shouting *safe* and the approving roar of the crowd, my father's voice always on top of everyone else's, washing over me.

Duncan's massive head bonked against my thigh, and he made a low whine. I didn't realize it until then, but I was crying.

"How did I become this man?" I asked, unsure if I was talking to Duncan or to myself, or if that mattered. He looked up at me.

"How do I *unbecome* this man?"

Duncan cocked his head to one side.

The all-too-familiar feelings of worthlessness and failure washed over me, but I kept them inside. Let them rush through me, leaving traces of their poison everywhere.

Duncan whined again.

If I wasn't in pain, I was deep in depression or having a panic attack. I couldn't sleep, had difficulty maintaining steady work after the Army, and had lost touch with my old troops. I couldn't keep them safe, couldn't bring them all home. Couldn't keep my wife happy or even remotely friendly toward me, and many of those feelings of worthlessness sloshing around inside me came from the words that tumbled from her mouth so carelessly on so many occasions.

Maybe if I'd been a better man, a better husband, she wouldn't have had the cause to say those things. But I don't know how I could have been better. If I'd been able to bring home her best friend's boyfriend from Afghanistan with me, maybe things between us would have remained strong.

But I wasn't better. I couldn't bring him home. Things didn't remain strong. I had failed at every task set in front of me.

Duncan let out a long, low growl. I pulled myself from the self-hate trance and looked down at him scowling at me.

"What?" I asked, defensively. "I did fucking fail. I failed at all of it."

Duncan growled again, barked, and then laid down at my feet, his ten-pound jaw resting on my toes. He whined and panted.

"You don't know what you're talking about," I said.

His eyes shot up to mine, and he let out a sharp growl that slowly softened as he placed his head back on my foot. He continued growling quietly, the vibration from it tickling my toes.

"I don't know what I could have done differently," I said. "For her or for them. I did everything I could think of. Put all of myself into it and came out of it every time with less of myself remaining."

I stared at the empty dugout for a long time, my mouth drying instantly at the thought of my adolescent cheek stuffed full of sunflower seeds, the spit-out shells crunching under everyone's cleated footsteps.

Duncan stood, and for the first time, walked away from me and tugged on his leash. I followed, and he slowly walked me over to the dugout I'd been staring at.

I sat on the metal bench and shuffled my feet in the dirt. Remnants of sunflower seed shells from a new generation were scattered about.

Duncan set his head on my lap, digging his muzzle into my belly, and rested there, still and silent.

In the background of my memory, I heard my teammates chanting at the opposing team's batters while rattling the dugout fencing.

There was one spring that our town hosted a baseball

camp on this field, and at the end of the week, we hosed down the last half of the third base line leading into home plate and took turns sliding in the mud into home base, the air crackling with energy, shouts of *safe* and bursts of laughter.

By then, I was weeping. At first, I was so overwhelmed by emotion I didn't understand what I was crying about until I had the time to realize I was crying about everything I'd ever kept to myself. Everything I'd ever repressed, and in that moment, I realized just how much there was.

Every hurt from childhood I swallowed in order to look strong, or to avoid being difficult. Every trigger pull that had ended a life. Every life that was impacted by that loss. Every piece of me that had died with every instance. All the pain, too vast and varied to list or even categorize without getting a headache. The divorce and the ocean of wrongdoing I'd swallowed with a smile. Everything I never wanted to burden others with and pretended to be competent in carrying alone poured out of me in an instant.

I wrapped my arms around Duncan's neck, rested my head on the top of his massive skull, and soaked the top of his head with tears.

Before, I felt like I had little to no support, like there was no one (except maybe this dog) to make me feel like I was worth something and deserved love, but no one knew I felt worthless. No one knew how long I stared into the shadows of my nightstand drawer. They knew I was getting divorced, but they got so few details. And I even kept many of my medical issues secret from people. Not because I needed them to be secrets, but just out of a misguided attempt to not burden others. No one could support me if no one knew I needed it, and no one would ever know I needed support if I swallowed every problem.

"I need help," I told Duncan when I finally caught my breath and stopped crying.

He raised his head and licked my face and hands, then nibbled at my ear and backed up quickly, like he was ready to play.

There was an old baseball with a few dingy red threads loose sitting in the dugout's corner. Duncan lunged for it, but I beat him to it and led him out of the dugout.

We were mostly fenced in—and he was too slow to get away from me anyway—so I unhooked his leash and tossed the ball into right field. He hustled his way over and ran back, dropping the slobbery ball at my feet in the dirt. I tossed it into left and then center field, then back to right, over and over again.

After a while, once Duncan's hustle became more of a stroll, I chased after him, tackling him in deep center field. He eagerly rubbed his back in the grass while I rubbed his belly, until we both stilled on our backs, watching the clouds change shape above us.

"You hungry, bud?"

Duncan's head jerked over to face me, one ear curiously lifted.

"Granola is definitely ready by now. I'm starving. You hungry too?" I stood up, slowly brushing away any grass left behind.

"Come on, let's get you some food."

That was the magic word. *Food.* Duncan popped up, suddenly full of energy again. I reattached his leash, and we walked back toward my parent's house. But I stopped him, took a knee, and put one arm around his massive neck. I caressed his cheek and scratched under his chin before planting a kiss on the top of his head.

"Thanks, buddy," I said. He gently nibbled the tip of my nose. I wiped his slobber from my face with a smile, and then we continued home

GRANOLA

3 cups oats
1 ½ cups walnuts, chopped
1 cup pecans, chopped
¾ cup almonds, sliced or slivered
¼ cup coconut oil
½ cup honey
1 TBSP light corn syrup
1/3 cup peanut butter
1 tsp vanilla

INSTRUCTIONS

Thoroughly mix oats and nuts. Preheat oven to 300°F. In a small saucepan over medium heat, melt oil, honey, peanut butter, and corn syrup. Bring to a low boil, stirring regularly. Cook for 2-3 minutes on low. Remove from heat and allow to cool for one minute before mixing in the vanilla. Pour over oat and nut mixture and thoroughly coat in sauce. Spread evenly over an ungreased cookie sheet. Bake for 12 minutes. Remove and thoroughly stir the granola, spread evenly again and place back in the oven. Bake 10 more minutes. Remove and let cool completely—DO NOT STIR AGAIN. Do not touch it until it is completely cooled. Break apart and store in an airtight container in the pantry/cabinet.
Time of year, humidity, and the type of cookie sheet you use can impact results. Experiment and find your sweet spot.

Great as cereal (especially with fresh blueberries), with ice cream, yogurt, or mix in peanuts, M&M's and dried cranberries for a hearty trail mix to snack on while walking your dog.

The Other Place
Novel Excerpt

CHAPTER 1

I saw the moment the universe collapsed, crumbled and reassembled to start again. Time bent and swayed. Location became irrelevant and light passed through endless oceans of black, like the distance from my hand to yours in a cramped room.

I could see all of time from this perspective; watch it become undone, forgotten, and impossible before being remade into your flawless skin, hair, laughter, and logic. Tendrils of pink mist and the glowing embers of what was swirled into the shape of you, giving form to all things.

Sensation and memory evaporated as I floated in a timeless chasm with a simple directive, like a compass, sewn into me. Always follow the mist, and always give whatever part of myself it required.

I peeled the paper lid from a half-and-half and dumped it

into my coffee, absentmindedly rubbing at my temple. At least a dozen empty single serving creamers lay scattered around the white bowl in front of me on the old Formica counters, the kind with the stainless-steel edging. The countertops had little flecks of gold in the design that lit up as the sun poured in through the front window.

A fleck of gold caught a reflection that pierced my retina and it started. A headache that turned everything in sight to pink mist and sent sparks scattering from the back of my neck to the top of my head.

The electricity settled, then leaked from my eyes, leaving jagged rivers of numbness down each cheek. The last time it happened, I got stuck in The Other Place, and it was weeks before I could remember my name.

"Want any more coffee?" a woman asked.

Her voice amplified and echoed inside me as one last spark skittered around beneath the skin under my left eye, then fizzled out.

"Huh?" I asked, rubbing the spot at the base of my skull where the headache generated from.

She raised her eyebrows, offered a little smile, and held up the coffeepot so I could see it better. The chestnut in her eyes was so familiar that it felt like looking in a mirror, before the familiarity was yanked away from me and she could have been anyone again.

"Oh," I said. "Please."

She filled my cup and said she'd get some more half-and-half before I ran out, then put the carafe back on the warmer and headed back in my direction as I emptied three creamers and half a pack of sugar into my coffee. As she neared, I noticed her name tag had a little smiley face on it that looked hand drawn with a marker next to the name *Clara*.

The door opened and more customers came in. A man and a little girl, maybe eight, who walked slowly through the door as if she carried a vast but invisible weight on her tiny shoulders. She wore a burgundy dress with a white collar and white buttons. Her hair was pulled back in a ponytail that was held in place by a chunky white bow. Her father held her hand as he patiently escorted her to the nearest booth.

I didn't know until then, but I was there to help the girl. After she walked through the door, a glowing pink mist surrounded her, like when one of those headaches came along. The light was gone as soon as I noticed it. It'd served its purpose, marking her. That's how I knew who needed me the most.

"Good morning," Clara said, beaming at the new arrivals, like she knew them well.

"It is now," the man said in return. He didn't turn to look at Clara when he said it, but you could hear the smile in his voice, and I liked him right away for no other reason than that.

"Do you know them?" I asked.

Clara hesitated, surveying me. "Yeah," she said, with a hint of joy and sadness in her tone. I cocked my head to one side curiously. She flushed, like I was digging into something personal, and I was about to apologize for prying when she responded.

"Sorry," she said. "I'm not used to talking personal stuff with strangers, but you seem nice. That's my brother and his girl, Riley. Wonderful kid."

"If he's your brother, I'm surprised he was so sweet to you when they came in."

She smiled widely. "He's adopted," she said, and we both laughed.

"That explains it." I emptied another creamer into my coffee.

"Riley's birthday is coming up. She's an Easter baby."

"Nice," I said, and then reluctantly added a question. "So what's wrong with her?"

Clara frowned. "What makes you ask that?"

"You just seemed sad talking about her." I paused. "And she was moving a little slowly, but she could just have a cold or something." The headache was gone, and I was myself again. My fingers tingled as we talked about Riley.

Clara nodded, but said nothing in response at first. Her eyes filled, but she took a breath and the waters receded. "She's been sick for a couple years, and not with a cold."

I nodded, drained my cup and asked for another refill. She obliged and then went over to Riley and her father's table to take their order.

I drank three more cups of coffee while waiting for them, my fingers buzzing, ready to work. Once they paid their bill, said their goodbyes, and left, I paid mine, thanked Clara, and started to follow Riley and her father outside, but stopped.

When I opened the door and the bell dinged, a tiny piece of a memory that seemed to involve Clara came and went before I could say what it was. I looked at her from the doorway. She watched me with the same confused expression I must have had. It seemed she was just about to say something along the lines of *Don't I know you from somewhere?*, as I was about to ask her the same, but that's when Riley and her father left my sight. So, I closed the door and followed them.

They walked together slowly down the uneven, broken sidewalk toward an apartment complex of four small brick buildings. All of them old, dingy rectangles with small windows, each covered with the same bars that matched the steel cages on every front door of the complex.

I gave them a few minutes to get settled in, and then went to their door and knocked. Since I didn't know them or their troubles, I couldn't have explained to anyone why I was trying to help them other than to say I felt compelled. I knew I had to follow them. Knew I had to knock on their door. Just like I knew I had to breathe. To blink. To eat. The compass inside me at work.

I wasn't gifted and wasn't in control of whatever power was in my possession. It was the payment of a debt I couldn't even comprehend. I didn't know who was collecting, why, or how long it would take to pay off that debt, but it was still a reality I couldn't dismiss or escape, even if I'd wanted to. For reasons I couldn't explain, it was the only place I could see myself at that moment in time, even if it ended up being the last place I ever saw.

The door opened. There was a living room inside the doorway to my right, with a small couch where Riley sat. I smiled at her and nodded.

"Can I help you?" her father asked.

"Actually, sir. I was hoping to help you."

He frowned. "I don't have any money," he said and started to close the door.

"That's not why I'm here," I said, and he stopped.

"Then why are you here?"

"Well—"

"Wait, I thought you looked familiar," he said. "Weren't you just at the Jolly Pirate? What do you want? Who sent you here?" He kept one hand on the door and placed the other on the door frame, effectively blocking my path, not that I would have tried to force my way in.

"No one sent me, and yes, I was just down the street at the Jolly Pirate. I saw you come in and could tell right away that *she* was someone I could help," I said, nodding toward Riley.

"What are you, some kind of faith healer? You got a church in the neighborhood?" Now he was full body blocking the entry and my view of Riley.

"No, sir. But not all faith healers are frauds. They just might not be using faith to heal."

He said nothing, just continued to survey me.

"She needs help, and I know you'd do anything to help her."

"You don't know anything about us," he said, taking a step closer to me.

"Am I wrong?" I asked, not retreating.

The man said nothing, but his facial expression was answer enough.

"I'm not promising you anything. I'm just asking for your permission to try. Ms. Riley's too," I added. "She needs to be OK with it as well."

"How'd you know her name?" he asked, his eyes like bullets.

"The waitress told me. Clara. Said how wonderful Riley was when I asked. That's all."

He instantly softened at the mention of his sister's name.

"You say you want to try," the man said. "Try what?"

"I just need to hold her hand for a few seconds."

"So you *are* a faith healer?"

"No, I'm John," I said, and held out my hand with the sudden realization that my name was one of my few remaining memories, but it wasn't the time to dwell on that.

"Erik," he said, and shook my hand, though it seemed to take a second for him to convince himself to do so. Couldn't blame him.

Riley nodded at me and smiled weakly. Her father looked at her, his eyes slowly filling with tears, like he couldn't stand to look at her without being swallowed by desperation. His expression was chaotic in an instant. There was so much love and hope. Sorrow and worry. His anxiety and obvious feelings of helplessness were palpable, and it suddenly became hard for me to breathe.

"It's OK, Daddy," Riley said, the words seeming to soothe him in a way my reassurances never would. "Just let him try. I'm so close now. What could it hurt?"

I didn't need to ask what she was so close to, and neither did Erik. He shook his head in protest, saying nothing at first.

"Don't talk like that," he finally choked out.

Riley stood and walked over to him slowly. She took his hand and guided him to the seat on the couch next to her, then rested her hand on his. "You're right, Daddy. Can he try? I'd like him to try."

After a moment, he nodded steadily, and I closed the door behind me, walked over to them, and took a knee in front of Riley.

"Let's not touch your dad right now," I said.

"Why not?" Erik asked, suddenly defensive again.

"Just don't want any mixed signals, is all," I said, offering no further explanation, not that I could. "No more talking now, OK, Erik? I need to focus on Riley."

He nodded and stayed quiet. Beads of sweat stood out on his forehead.

"What should I do?" Riley asked, calm as a sniper.

I shook my head. "Not a thing. I'm just going to take your hand in mine and have a little look around. If I can find what's hurting you, I might be able to just soak it up."

"Like a sponge?" she asked, her voice dreamy.

"Yes, angel. Like a sponge," I whispered, my own voice taking on dreamy qualities. I took her hand in mine and closed my eyes, focusing.

All I knew for sure was, when I did this, some part of me went to The Other Place and not all of me came back. Even though I no longer remembered why I would give an unknown part of myself to a stranger, it felt right to do it for Riley in the same way it would have felt right to do it for someone I loved unconditionally. Besides, she didn't feel like a stranger, in the same way the waitress, Clara, had seemed familiar to me before. Maybe it was just their kindness that made them both feel a little like home.

The air between us seemed too thin, and the temperature dropped. Sensing a faint glimmer of light in the room, I opened my eyes. Some of the pink mist floated between us. Riley sat calmly in front of me. Erik was still there, in a way, but only as a shadow compared to Riley, who glowed. Her eyes were closed, and her head tilted to one side, a quizzical frown on her delicate forehead. The light from Riley brightened, and my eyes burned. I tried to close them again, but couldn't.

As soon as I tightened my grip on her hand, my vision fractured like a mirror; everything around me breaking apart. Each piece of the splintering world refracted light differently, sending pieces of each of us and the surrounding room into different locations. There was a sinking feeling in my stomach, like I was falling until enough of the pink mist could seep through the gaps between pieces and pull me through to The Other Place. The place where healers go to wring out the sickness they've absorbed.

Pink curtains flowing up to an endless ceiling formed a narrow hallway in front of me. A sliver of light leaked through a panel down the path, and I started toward it. The ground moaned quietly with each step, as if I walked in a cemetery where the dead weren't quite dead yet and tried to writhe their way back to the surface.

Beyond the curtains was the sound of overlapping voices in languages I'd never heard. A metallic clanging that rose, fell, and echoed, like percussion symbols tumbling down concrete steps. The smell of flesh and other things, not dishes or ingredients, but things indecipherable to me. Things that squealed behind the roar of flames and clanging metal.

Because Riley had been calm, I was calm. It was her death being deposited here, and I reached for the gap in the curtains eagerly, as if she were mine to save and not just some stranger's child.

It was a dining hall like many I'd seen before, only the roof was glass, and beyond that, a bright swirl of pink embers cut through a black sky filled with more stars than I'd ever seen. Chattering people crammed every table, all wearing the same pristine beige suits, with white masks that were blank except for a red hole where mouths should have been.

They all had bowls of smiling human faces in a chunky, milk-like substance. The faces laughed until the noise was overwhelming. All the diners blended the smiles and laughter with mixer hands that brought a sudden silence to the room until the diners slurped their soup through the masks.

As the gulping echoed throughout the dining hall, each corner of the room developed its own towering dark red waterfall. People stood by the thousands at each of the beaches surrounding the waterfalls. At what appeared to be timed intervals, one person after another fell into the red liquid, swam toward the fall, and stood there, letting it deposit directly into their gaping mouths at an extreme velocity, until, eventually, they went under.

From above the waterfall, giant humanoids with insect limbs ripped trees from the ground and tossed them down, taking out anyone wading in too sluggishly. Every time it hit a group, they roared with approval.

A hand fell on my shoulder. As I turned to see who was there, the room brightened, and the burning pink mist in the sky pulsed above me. Before I saw who it was, I was back in the hallway of pink curtains, being pulled by an invisible force toward a door, my feet scuffing the ground with the moaning dead below.

I never remembered what happened when I went looking for sickness inside someone. It was like something else took control for a while. Maybe my mind blocked it out automatically; like it was too much. An information overload. My debtor blocking access to understanding.

There was something about a mirror breaking in the back of my mind and a hand on my shoulder, but that's all I could salvage from whatever happened.

I felt electricity, crackling static, from somewhere deep inside. That sensation intensified until a massive weight hit me in the center of the chest, and I was pushed away from Riley, falling back against the door.

Her burden was more than I expected.

I gasped for breath, slowly pushing myself into a sitting position against their door. After a moment, I stood and brushed off my pants and shirtsleeves. My heart and breathing slowed, and my vision returned to normal.

Riley looked like a regular kid again. The color in her cheeks had returned, and the sunken expression in her eyes was gone. Erik looked back and forth between us frantically.

"She's fine now, Erik," I said.

He looked at her, and she nodded cheerfully, without hesitation.

"It's gone, Daddy."

His face contorted momentarily, then returned to uncertainty and panic. "Are you sure?" He trembled everywhere, holding her shoulder a little too tightly. "How do you know?" he asked, looking back and forth between us again.

Riley shrugged, and Erik's arms dropped into his lap. She took his face in her hands but looked at me. "I can't explain it." She paused and frowned. "I don't think he can either," she said, and I confirmed her suspicions with silence. She looked at her father and continued. "I just know. You don't have to worry about me anymore. At least, not about this."

The greatest weight Erik had ever carried had just been unexpectedly lifted from his shoulders, and I saw the physical manifestation of him becoming unburdened. I would never get over the sight of such complete and overwhelming relief surprising a person in such a way. It made everything worthwhile, even though I had no idea what everything really meant. Not yet.

Riley stood and walked toward me. Erik shouted a desperate protest, like he thought if we touched again, she'd go back to dying.

"It's OK, Erik. Doesn't go both ways."

She took my hand and gave it a little tug, so I kneeled to be face-to-face with her. As she hugged me for a long time, neither of us spoke. She pulled back from me, took the white bow from her hair, and held it out.

"Here," she said. "So you don't forget me. I've got a drawer full of them anyway."

"I would never be able to forget you, but thanks." I took the bow and stood.

Riley smiled up at me at first, but then her expression changed to confusion.

"What is it?" I asked.

She frowned hard, considering. "Something is hurting you too," she said. "I could feel it...kind of. It's not even really hurting you...it's just. I don't know. I can't explain it."

"What do you mean?" I asked. "Is it a sickness like what

was in you?"

"No," she said right away. "Nothing like that. It's not a person making you do things either, not really, but kind of?"

"Making me do things?"

She shook her head but said nothing. It was clear I'd get nothing further from her, and she was already looking like she was forgetting what we were talking about. So I just shrugged, smiled, and told her to take care of her dad.

When I opened the door and stepped out, Erik unglued himself from the couch, came over, and stood beside his daughter, one hand on her shoulder. To say he looked confused would be an understatement.

"How?" was all he could manage.

"Does it matter?"

After a moment, he shook his head. "I don't know how I can ever thank you properly."

"Your sister told me Riley's birthday is coming up. Just make it special for her, and I'll consider us even," I said and held out my hand. We shook, and I winked at Riley, nodded at Erik, and walked back toward the donut shop to get my car.

Before I turned the corner, I looked back. Erik held Riley tight, both of them watching me leave. I waved, and they waved back. As I turned the corner, Erik let out a whooping cry of joy that caused the hair on my arms to stand up. He said, "We've got to call Clara," and then I heard their door close.

Jordan earned an MFA in Creative Writing from Miami of Ohio. His non-fiction essay Lost Time: A Road Trip Journal was published in Adelaide Literary Magazine, February 2019. His debut novel, White Oaks, was a finalist in the Ohio Writer's Associations' Great Novel Contest of 2019 before being published by Running Wild Press October 2022. His second novel, Drone, a science fiction satire about the friendship between a sentient military drone and a refugee boy during an environmental apocalypse, will be released in the summer of 2026. He lives and works in Columbus Ohio.

You can find him on Instagram @JordanDanKing

N
+
S

Illumination of Conscience

September 1878

The foul mood assaulted Novak when he entered the workshop. Tools flung to the benches with contempt. Drawers slammed shut. Men spoke in hushed whispers instead of open chatter. A young mucker crashed into him on his way to the stairs, but hurried off without so much as an "excuse me," a "sorry," or a "thank you," when Novak had helped him gather the scattered diagrams and reports.

Novak only responded with a shrug. He couldn't blame the kid—Joseph, if memory served. He joined recently after graduating from university, and the poor boy still hadn't learned the ropes. The laboratory employed dozens of *muckers*—their name for the small army of subordinate inventors, engineers, and technicians who filled any kind of role or expertise that might be needed. They also trudged through the muck to spare the great minds above them the inconvenience of getting their hands dirty. In Novak's six years of working here, he'd never managed to scrub the grime from under his fingernails.

He shuffled to his workstation and trudged up the stairs to his worktable on the mezzanine. It was cluttered with the broken remains of last night's failed and half-finished projects. His bench mate, Elias, pushed them into a haphazardly teetering pile on Novak's side of the desk. Sweeping them all into the rummage bin and ignoring Elias's dirty look, Novak plopped into his seat with a sigh. At least last night, he'd had the prudence to enter his findings into the lab notebook before all the figures and observations tumbled out of his tired mind. He should have finished tidying up before he left for the evening. It had been nine-thirty after all.

They had all been working late to deliver results on the latest filaments, but precious little good that did any of them. Another dozen trials had come and gone with middling success. The longest burning lamp lasted only six hours and five minutes. Not long enough.

This Tuesday had dawned dismal and sweaty, and Novak had already loosened his tie by the time he reached the shop at half-past eight, half-past *late*.

A paper sat open on the desk, a copy of the *Sun*, already stained by coffee rings. The date at the top showed it was the sixteenth. He didn't bother reading further.

Now Novak understood the reason for the paranoia and unrest in the office. *Of course!* The long-dreaded day had finally arrived. In the haze of long evenings and early mornings, he'd almost forgotten.

Today, the Wizard returned.

As if heralded by a clap of thunder, an office door slammed open, and out stormed Prospero himself. "I have it now, men!"

Novak stifled a groan. The man possessed far too much energy for this hour. His deep-set, wrinkled eyes glowed with excitement. He wore an impeccable suit and bow tie, his whitening hair combed over his head, but his eyebrows stayed black and bushy. A dangerous smirk twisted his lips, the kind of grin that held ideas of the most terrible kind.

"During my trip to Ansonia, Connecticut, I discovered the most incredible device, and procured the rights and building permits for William Wallace's telemachon. This generator can provide enough energy to power our electrical work for the entirety of not only this workshop but also Menlo Park!"

He gave a dramatic pause for effect, met only with blank half-asleep stares and anticipatory anxiety before moving on. "The parts and schematics will be delivered in a fortnight, and we will begin construction immediately. When it arrives, I want a team of twenty men to start building. Any volunteers? Charles, I want you leading this project."

Novak slunk in his seat. As much as he tired of filaments, he knew he didn't want to work with *Charles*. A few hands raised, Elias's included. But when the volunteers didn't meet the requested quota, the lead recruited his pick of the unwilling lot, like a team captain on the playground choosing sides for a baseball team. He rattled off several names, working his way around the room.

When he called the name *Joseph*, four different muckers stood, and Charles pointed at the one who'd dropped his papers earlier. He was a young man with pale skin, straight dark hair cut in a neat style, a large hooked nose, and a nervous demeanor. He wore a white striped, checkered shirt, a brown checked vest, and a brown striped tie, but eschewed the suit jackets of his older coworkers.

"Joseph Harris," he said, wringing his hands. "I work on magneto-electric machines."

"You'll do." Joseph sank back into his seat with a sigh as Charles moved on, scanning toward Novak's desk. Since Elias had already volunteered, maybe he could get away with—

"…and Novak!" Charles called.

Novak pasted on a grin and raised his hand in acknowledgment, but internally, he braced himself as the boss spoke again.

"Now I'll be hiring contractors to erect a new machine

shop in the rear area of the laboratory. You'll be assembling the telemachon there. This will be connected to the laboratory, and to the green outside, in parallel circuits. It will be installed by early December in preparation for a grand public exhibition."

Voices murmured. This was the first any of them heard about an exhibition. Seldom a week passed without some reporter sticking their cameras and pens in their business, asking for a personal tour, or an interview with the boss, but an *exhibition*? What kind of pressure would that elicit from the public?

The boss spoke again once the chatter died, his voice stern as a drill sergeant. "Everyone will be expected to keep up with their existing work in addition to this project, and we're doubling phonograph production. What's the most recent filament record? Our target is ten hours, correct?"

Nobody answered, unwilling to be the bearer of bad news.

"Huh? *What is it?*" the boss demanded.

"Six hours and five minutes," Novak offered finally. "Sir, we made this new record last night, up from four hours and twenty-nine minutes."

"I want development to find one that hits twenty within the end of the month. The world is looking to us as a beacon of innovation! Let's get to work, men."

With that, the great Edison spun on his heel and returned to his office with Charles, slamming the door behind him. The murmurs turned into a cacophony of voices, as everyone had something to say to their neighbor about the new announcement.

"A new project on top of our work?"

"We're already doing overtime!"

"An exhibition during the holidays?"

"What do we have to exhibit? Boxes of broken bulbs!"

"Doubling phonograph production! We're barely meeting orders!"

Novak simply put his head in his hands and rubbed his

temples where a migraine was already forming. The young muckers could have their outrage. He'd worked with Edison long enough to know the man's ridiculous timetables and cruel conditions. While little surprised him anymore, this set of constraints struck a new egregious record. The prospect of endless overtime and early mornings turned his already tired bones to lead.

Elias leaned over to Novak and gently touched his elbow. "Are you alright there?"

"Never worse," Novak grumbled.

"Come now, don't speak like that here." Elias glanced over his shoulder toward the office. Charles would probably emerge any moment with a new stack of demands.

"I've earned the right to speak any way I please." Novak lifted his head from his hands and leaned back in his chair, crossing his arms with a scowl. Nobody was too important for Edison to sack, but after six years of dutifully putting up with the madman's audacity, Novak was about as close as a mucker could get to being a permanent fixture of the workshop.

Given that Edison had sold all his manufacturing concerns in Newark to move to the Menlo Park workshop earlier that year, that was saying something.

Elias sighed. "For what it's worth, I'm glad you were selected for the project too. We'll need your electrical expertise if we want to have any hope of getting this monster up and running."

"Why did you volunteer so quickly then?"

"It's an *opportunity*, Novak."

The banging office door interrupted Elias before he could bloviate on the virtues of burning the midnight oil. He ducked his head like an ashamed schoolboy caught passing notes as Charles strode out, carrying a stack of assignments, reports, and timetables.

Novak rolled his eyes but reached for his lab notebook, nonetheless.

"I'll elaborate if you want to meet at Linwood Grove for

a drink after work," Elias muttered, talking out of the corner of his mouth as he made himself look busy preparing a new set of filaments for testing.

"That sounds like a fair deal. You owe me one for dragging me into this project."

"For the record, I dragged you into no such thing."

Novak allowed himself a halfhearted grin as Elias handed him the prepared filament, but he quickly curbed his enthusiasm when Charles finished circling his rounds to drop the new schedule on their desk.

He didn't need to look at the paper to know he wouldn't be getting that drink until long after the dinner rush had meandered home.

Novak and Elias walked to Linwood Grove together in silence. The warmth of the September day had given way to a chill night, and Novak welcomed the brisk breeze as a reprieve from the stuffy, stale air of the workshop. Though it was a short walk to the tavern where they would debrief the events of the day together, they maintained an unspoken agreement to keep these sacred minutes to themselves.

In the soft glow of the gas lamps, Novak considered just what they were trying to accomplish. As his shadow shortened, disappeared beneath his feet, then stretched behind him as he passed each light, he considered the paths the wires would need to trace beneath the ground to each and every post. As he watched the fire flicker through the glass, he reflected on how the filament would need to burn long and steady, without needing replacement. His mind jumbled with the materials and properties listed and crossed out in his notebooks and scattered all over his desk. Carbon fiber, platinum, cotton, linen, wood, or paper? What shape? What size?

As he turned a corner and noticed one gas lamp hadn't been lit, he wondered how many lamplighters he might put out of a job, if by some miracle, they succeeded in this scheme.

What might the world look like if they could light the night with electric lights? Hundreds could be lit and extinguished with the simple flip of a switch.

Those thoughts snuffed out as easily as a candle. Such concerns belonged to the realm of Edison's promises, which kept investors' money flowing steadily into his coffers. What didn't pay for material costs, telemachons, and meager salaries stayed firmly in the master's grip. Once, Novak might have dreamed of mechanical wonders, of invention for invention's sake, and the pursuit of knowledge out of sheer curiosity. He'd sacrificed such motivation in pursuit of different goals long ago. If the Wizard of Menlo Park dreamed of anything, Novak believed he only dreamed of fame. Journal entries. Exhibitions.

Soon enough, the pair arrived at the Linwood Grove Tavern. It would close soon, so they hurried to the bar and put in their orders. Once settled in with their drinks, Elias broke the comfortable silence, and the dignified persona he put on while on the job.

"Goddamn that tyrant," he said, wiping his mouth after a long swig.

"Cheers to that." Novak clinked his glass to Elias's still raised one and took a drink of his beer. "But you still volunteered."

"We need the money with another baby on the way, and the long hours will pay."

"But won't your wife need you at home?"

Elias grimaced. "It's bad enough with the current hours. I wish I had the chance to talk it over with Emily, but knowing Charles…"

"…He'd never let you onto the project if you didn't jump on right away, and it's too good of an *opportunity* to pass up," Novak finished the thought for him.

"Exactly."

"She'll understand if you're doing this for the good of the family."

"She will, she's a good woman." Elias's haggard face

softened as he thought of his sweetheart at home. Novak had met Emily a few times before. He'd seen how happy they were together, and celebrated their union, despite his own secret heartbreak. Novak leaned back in his seat to stretch his back, achy from curling over his workbench all day. Out of the corner of his eye, he noticed a familiar figure sitting at the other end of the bar, eating a late dinner; one of the few other patrons at this hour of the night.

"Joseph Harris, right?" he called to the lonely diner.

"Oh! Uh." Joseph lifted his head and met Novak's eyes, making it obvious that he'd been listening and trying not to get caught. "Sorry, sir, didn't mean to bother you."

"Might as well sit with us if you're going to eavesdrop," Elias offered with a friendly wave.

Joseph sheepishly shrugged his shoulders and shuffled down a couple of seats with his tray. "Didn't follow you sirs. Just came for supper. You actually walked in a few minutes after I did. This is one of the only places open late enough to grab some food after work."

"Forgot to pack your dinner?" Elias said sympathetically.

"Do you always pack one?"

"You should start," Novak grumbled. "We'll be working through supper every day for the next four months."

Joseph responded by scarfing down a bite of his sandwich and pulling a newspaper out of his knapsack. "Did you see our headline today?"

"Did we get *another* one?" Novak asked.

"I read it this morning. Left it on the desk for you," Elias said, shrugging.

"The boss is always babbling to the press. Usually before we hear anything about his announcements. I care not anymore." Novak crossed his arms, but leaned over to scan the headlines.

"*Edison's Newest Marvel. Sending cheap light, heat, and power by electricity*," Joseph read aloud, shifting so Novak could read over his shoulder. "*Mr. Edison says that he has discovered how to make electricity a cheap and practicable substitute for illuminating gas. Many scientific men have worked assiduously in that direction, but with little success. A powerful electric light was the result of these experiments, but the problem of its division into many small lights was a puzzler. Gramme, Siemens, Brush, Wallace, and others produced at most ten lights from a single machine, but a single one of them was found to be impracticable for lighting aught save large foundries, mills, and workshops. It has been reserved for Mr. Edison to solve the difficult problem desired. This, he says, he has done within a few days… Mr. Edison, besides his power of organization, has the faculty for developing the ideas and mechanical construction of others."*

THE SUN, MONDAY, SEPTEMBER 16, 1878.

EDISON'S NEWEST MARVEL.

SENDING CHEAP LIGHT, HEAT, AND POWER BY ELECTRICITY.

Illuminating Gas to be Superseded—Edison Solving the Problem of Dividing the Too Great Brilliancy from an Electric Machine.

Mr. Edison says that he has discovered how to make electricity a cheap and practicable substitute for illuminating gas. Many scientific men have worked assiduously in that direction, but with little success. A powerful electric light was the result of these experiments, but the problem of its division into many small lights was a puzzler. Gramme, Siemens, Brush, Wallace, and others produced at most ten lights from a single machine, but a single one of them was found to be impracticable for lighting aught save large foundries, mills, and workshops. It has been reserved for Mr. Edison to solve the difficult problem desired. This, he says, he has done within a few days. His experience with the telephone, however, has taught him to be cautious, and he is exerting himself to protect the new scientific marvel, which, he says, will make the use of gas for illumination a thing of the past.

Novak groaned. "These papers, they worship the very dust the man walks on."

"They're right about the last point at least," Elias said defensively, "If it weren't for his authority to gather us all in one place, we couldn't accomplish half the work we do. His connections are something we lack, and at the very least, the man keeps us employed in the pursuit of science. There's some credit to be given where credit is due."

"What few original ideas he shares are eclipsed by his overbearing personality and misunderstanding of scientific pursuit. One cannot simply *will* a working filament into existence by scowling at it. You must discover them through careful experimentation and iteration!"

"Novak, yes, yes, we know." Elias put a gentle hand on his shoulder and turned to Joseph. "I apologize you'll have to work with my grouch of a friend. He's normally not this prickly."

"Of course I'm always prickly," Novak protested, but he lowered his defenses and gave Joseph a slight smile to let the younger man know he was only joking. After a dozen or more similar articles about his own work, without the slightest mention of his name along with Mr. Edison's, he couldn't bring himself to care less. All the same, he couldn't bring himself to ruin Joseph's night either, so he kept his mouth shut as the other two continued chatting.

Elias ignored his comment. "You should be excited to see your first feature. I remember I was."

Joseph folded up the paper to return to his bag. "I understand. Been working for four months now, but I've barely said two words to Mr. Edison since he hired me. The other muckers told me Mr.... I'm sorry, I don't know how to pronounce your last name."

Nobody knows how to pronounce his Serbian last name, so he brushes it aside. "Just call me Novak. Enough with the *sir* and the *mister* nonsense. We are equals now, eh? You have a degree, do you not?"

"I'm a mechanical engineer, yes sir—Novak. Well,

I heard that you were responsible for a great number of innovations on the telegraph patents."

Novak grins at the recognition. "Indeed. At least the last hundred of them. You and I, we will look out for each other."

"Thank you, Novak. I'm happy to help." Joseph shook his hand with a grin. "The same regards to you too, Elias."

"Thank you, Joseph." Elias smiled, but it didn't quite reach his eyes as the weariness settled back over his shoulders. "I should get going, it's late."

"I understand. Family first," Novak said.

"Take care."

"Have a good night!"

Elias slid his empty glass across the bar to the keeper, paid for both men, and the two left together, meandering through the park under the gas lamps.

"Do you have family to be getting home to?" Novak asked Joseph once they made it outside.

"Not here. I'm the oldest of four boys, who all live back home with Ma and Pa. I'm the first in our family to go to college."

"Good for you. They must be proud."

"They are. Use me as an example for my brothers to hit the books, though. Right now, I live with some college mates who also found jobs around the area, but I'm hoping to bring my girl, Jenna, to live out with me eventually. Soon as we get married, that is."

"Oh?"

"She's my childhood sweetheart. I'm planning on proposing to her in a couple months, soon as I make enough to afford a ring. That's part of why I'm excited about this project. Aside from the work itself."

"You and Elias have a lot in common."

"He seems like a good guy."

Novak smiled and nodded, reminiscing on his and Elias's years of friendship both inside and outside of the professional sphere. When he'd first applied for the job at the workshop and made the passage across the Atlantic, Edison had accepted him for the role. But when he'd arrived for the first day of work, the supervisor, Charles, had blocked him from the building and refused to believe or take his credentials. Elias had been new at the time, but he'd taken pity on the foreigner and risked his own job to sneak Novak into the building for an audience with Edison to clear up the issue. Charles came down hard on him after that, but Novak got the job. At work, they avoided speaking to each other, lest they appear too friendly, and Elias bowed to Charles and Edison, where Novak had never gotten over that particular grudge. But outside of the laboratory, Elias had remained Novak's closest ally and advocate in the hard years that followed.

"Yes, he is a good man indeed," Novak confirmed.

"I'm glad I ran into you tonight."

"Well, for better or for worse, you're stuck with the both of us for the time being."

"For better, I think, Novak." Joseph grinned and stopped in the path. "This is my turn. I'll see you tomorrow!"

"Bright and early."

"Don't ya know it." Joseph laughed before waving and taking his leave.

Novak stood still for a minute, watching him depart, before turning and making his way back to his house. It was a modest dwelling, a little two-story house with a postage-stamp sized backyard overgrown from disuse, but one he was proud to call his own. He let himself in quietly, and sighed as he lit a few lamps to illuminate the living room. Coming across the ocean with nothing but his hard-won education, he'd worked diligently to furnish the place over the last several years. A patterned rug, an armchair, and his old steamer trunk that served as a coffee table, which was currently stacked high with unread books. He'd meant to build or buy a shelf eventually, but time had run away from him. A few trappings from home hung on the wall. Icons, a crucifix, a cuckoo clock his father had made ranked among his most treasured possessions. He stopped at the secretary desk in the corner, where his gaze lingered over a stack of letters and mementos. Feathers, pressed flowers, little painted cards. He'd kept all the letters from a long string of correspondence. The next letter wouldn't come for another week or two. Even with the telegraphs he'd worked so hard on, passage across the continents was slow, and sending messages was so expensive, especially for Sonja.

Loneliness had struck once again when Novak had heard Elias speak of his family. Joseph had his sweetheart close, even if he needed to visit the next state to see her. At least they could look forward to their engagement. In such times, Novak couldn't help but indulge his jealousy. Six years. It had been six years since he'd left his beloved wife, Sonja, and their infant son Mirko. He sank into his desk chair and let his fingers brush the picture he kept pinned to the inside of the desk. While he might have a mind for the sciences, his wife possessed the artistic skill between them. He'd fallen in love with her intense focus while she sketched in the meadows of their village. In each of her letters, she included some drawing or another, but this was his favorite. It showed his son, now a young boy, chasing butterflies and laughing. In just a few pen strokes, she'd captured the joy in his expression, the way his curls bounced as he ran, how his chubby little hands grasped for the fragile insect but never quite caught the evasive colorful creature.

A tear splattered onto the wood. He didn't wipe it away as the waves of homesickness washed over him. When the letter of acceptance had come from abroad, he'd almost refused to take it, but Sonja had encouraged him to follow his dreams to America. They would follow soon. He'd been fooled by the newspapers acclaiming Mr. Edison's excellence. Facing the treasures he'd left behind, his achievements meant nothing.

His boy had grown up without his papa.

Novak's pain doubled as he reread Sonja's last letter about

another hard drought that had killed their crops. They would have trouble paying off their bills at the end of the year without him there to support them. But without fail, she put on a brave face through her words, pretending she had the situation under control and that she would find a solution, somehow. She ended her letter as she always did.

"I miss you dearly, but I love you, and I am proud. We will see each other again."

Novak reconsidered Elias and Joseph's words about the project, the hours, the money. With the press of a secret switch, he opened a hidden compartment in the desk and pulled out a drawer where he kept a store of cash. He counted it, counted it again, then scribbled some calculations on the back of a used envelope.

It all added up.

He didn't want to get his hopes up, so he checked his math, recounted the money, then leaned back in his chair and took a deep breath.

Maybe this could work.

He removed a blank sheet of paper from the pile and wrote:

My dearest Sonja and Mirko,

My apologies for writing so soon after the last letter. I scarcely remember the contents of the last missive, but I have exciting news to share. There's been a new project announced at work, one that will give me more hours and more pay. I will be able to afford tickets for your passage across the Atlantic in just a few months.

Make all the necessary arrangements to sell the house and property and travel to America by Christmastime. When the money arrives, sail from the port of Dubrovnik to Palermo, where a ship will take you through the Strait of Gibraltar into the open ocean. This part of the voyage will be the hardest, but at long last, you will reach Ellis Island, where you will go through immigration. After that, make your way to Menlo Park, New Jersey, by train.

I will enclose maps and directions with this letter. Travel safe, but make haste. If you can make it to America by the holiday, we at the laboratory may have a spectacular surprise for you. The Wizard is working on a magic show of electric lights, and your Papa will be a part of it.

I miss you, but I love you, and I am proud. We will see each other again.

Hopefully, very soon.
Novak

As he set down his pen, Novak allowed himself to hope for the first time in years. He prepared himself for bed and extinguished his gas lamps. Even as he drifted to sleep, alone and exhausted, dreading work in the morning with all of his being, he slipped the envelope onto his nightstand, and dreamed of the sea.

October 1878

Despite the twelve-hour workdays and the constant harassment from Charles, Novak let nothing stand in the way of his goal. The generator shipped from Connecticut in numerous wooden crates packed with straw and sawdust. The contractors started construction on the extension to the workshop, which would not be completed for some weeks. In the meantime, the work would have to be partially completed in the laboratory. This meant clearing space by shoving every other operation into nooks and crannies, much to the chagrin of those workers who now sat on each other's laps, elbowing one another in the face as they tried to accomplish their tasks.

The team Charles formed worked in shifts to unpack, organize, and assemble each part when it arrived. They would build what they could manage indoors, then move the completed pieces outside once the new construction was complete, and finish connecting them there. But as the shifts turned over the work to each other, the space gradually shrank as the generator's guts sprawled over the floor of the workshop. Soon, there was barely room to tiptoe around the mechanical leviathan. Novak spent hours squatting on the tarp, precariously posed between gears and disconnected levers, puzzling with Joseph over schematics.

He slipped on grease more times than he'd like to admit to Elias.

Though the parts came labeled, the nomenclature didn't match the instructions, and the worst of the problems arrived when tags went missing. A stack of orphaned components left concerning gaps in the assembly, and the afternoon shift denied any responsibility for the unidentifiable items.

As the problems escalated, Charles's temper worsened. At first, he simply kept everyone to a strict timetable, rushing the workers to finish a certain number of parts by the end of each day, and complaining bitterly if they fell behind. But when Elias approached him to point out the issues and ask for guidance, the man flipped a switch. He hovered over every joint, rivet, and hinge, instructing the muckers how to put the machine together. Joseph endured the unenviable position as the youngest on their team, but he was twenty-four, not four. Yet Charles treated him as if he didn't know the business end of a hammer. If he made a section of the apparatus, Charles would inevitably sweep in after him to disassemble and redo it in his own fashion, though neither Novak nor Elias found any fault in Joseph's original design. Novak did his best to distract the supervisor from his protégé, bitterly remembering the days when he had fallen subject to the same scrutiny.

Novak tried to ignore Charles, and only pretended to fiddle with a loose bolt as he surveyed the mess that they'd made of the project. Given the blueprints sent by the manufacturer, his knowledge of electromagnetic study and mechanics, and the state of the assembly so far, he identified several fatal errors in the first couple of steps that perpetuated through the later steps of building. Nobody had noticed them at the start. Instead, they'd simply forged ahead and hoped it would come together in the end.

Charles came up behind Novak again and snatched the plans out of his hands.

"Novak! How many times do I have to tell you to do your job?"

Novak didn't look up from his problem. How much damage had they unwittingly done to the machine? Could the project be salvaged given its current state?

"Are you stupid, man?" He spoke slowly and over-enunciated each word, as if Novak couldn't understand English. "Put. That. Magneto. In. There."

If Novak did as Charles instructed, the conductors could short and cause an arc flash. The huge electrical explosion would endanger all the operators. Novak slowly shook his head and turned over the part in his hand.

"I am the head engineer. Are you questioning my judgment?" Charles spewed. He grabbed the magneto out of Novak's hand and waved it in his face.

"I think this project was rushed and could stand a second inspection," Novak said carefully, gesturing at the schematic in Charles's hand.

Charles shoved the magneto into the machine. Backward. "We do not have *time*—"

Novak snapped. He'd had enough of this man's condescension and ineptitude. He tore the magneto back out of the machine and returned it in the proper orientation. "We must rip this machine apart piece by piece and repair several *major* issues before it humiliates all of us, or worse, kills someone. Look at this mess: unstable couplings, backward coiling, shorted circuits! You even put the magnetos in with reversed polarity. I haven't even looked over the boiler!"

"Mr. Edison did not appoint *you* to be the head of this project! I can assure you I have personally overseen every inch of this apparatus."

That's what I'm afraid of, Novak thought.

"I can assure you it will function as planned. We do not have the time to rip it apart piece by piece, and we are behind enough on schedule already. That's a ridiculous suggestion. If you're so concerned about the couplings and coiling and circuits, you can stay late to check them over yourself. Congratulations."

Novak glowered at Charles as the man stalked off and slammed the door of his office. He would already be staying late to watch over the lightbulb, so it would be a productive use of time to go over the machine himself, without the meddling middle manager in his way. Elias came over to him and put a comforting hand on Novak's shoulder.

"I'll try to talk some sense into him."

Novak shook off Elias's hand with a shrug. "Do not waste your time. The man is too stubborn to listen to good sense."

"I'll *try*," Elias repeated, before making his way to the office to face the ogre inside.

The end of the morning shift came as a welcome relief for all. Novak took a stroll around the park to clear his head, and ate his lunch in sullen silence.

In the afternoons when the trio didn't labor over the generator, they studied the filaments. Novak constructed a matrix on a corkboard out of strips of paper and string, all neatly arranged. Each row represented a different filament material, each column a unique method of preparation, and each intersection would hold the data for that test. It took a week of argument and analysis to design the initial experiment. Elias and Novak carefully chose their most promising combinations, and Joseph recorded, clipped, and pinned each one to the board.

Next came the long, long hours of watching and recording. They twisted the fibers into shape, loaded them into the bulbs, used pumps to create vacuums, and checked every seal for defects. Then came the moment of truth: energizing the wire. Novak let Joseph have the honor of flipping the first switch. The electrical wires buzzed, the light flickered to life, and he gasped in delight as its soft steady light illuminated their small portion of the workshop.

A soft hope flickered to life in Novak's heart as well. Maybe this could be the right one.

They set up a row of the bulbs in a parallel circuit and prepared the next round of filaments while they waited for the current tests to burn out. This became their habit for the following days, and the corkboard matrix gradually devolved into a mess of scrapped ideas and desperate attempts. As the evenings stretched on, Elias monitored the lights, and Novak took notes on their performance. On the thirty-first, eventually, Elias bid his friends goodnight to return home to his wife and children, leaving Joseph on duty with Novak, who kept his post. The laboratory steadily emptied until Edison finally emerged from his office, the last to leave the building.

The man looked haggard and drawn in the stark light of the electric lamps as he locked his office door behind him. Novak averted his gaze, fixing his attention on the game of hangman he was playing with Joseph. Damn kid always beat him. Silly English spellings.

Instead of walking out the front door of the laboratory, the boss's footsteps clicked up the metal stairs of the mezzanine. Joseph quickly pulled a stray scrap of paper over their game to hide the fact that their hangman looked an awful lot like Charles. Novak spun around on his stool and stood on creaky bones to greet the man who held all of their livelihoods in the palm of his hand.

"Working late again tonight, boys?" Edison asked.

"Yes, sir. We'll be taking shifts sleeping, and Elias will come in early tomorrow," Joseph explained.

"Ah, very good. What's the filament on this one?"

"Carbonized cotton, sir."

"Wasn't that one of the first we tried?"

"It was, but out of all the variations we have tried—

platinum, carbon steel, untreated cotton, linen, and other fibers—this was the best result. We are verifying the shape again and trying different carbonization methods," Novak explained.

"I see. How long has it run?"

"This one began at two-thirty today. It is now…" Novak fumbled for the time. Edison pulled a fine silver pocket watch out of his pants pocket and held it up to the incandescent light.

"Quarter to ten."

Novak did the quick math in his head. "So it has been seven hours, fifteen minutes, and counting. Beating our past record." He located his watch in his desk's clutter, then scribbled down the value in tally marks so he could continue counting.

"Very well then. Keep up the good work, men." The Wizard gave them a rare smile, and reached into his pocket to pull out a wallet. He pulled out two one-dollar bills and handed one to each of them. "You'll be paid overtime for the night, but here's a tip if you want to get a late-night snack from Linwood Grove."

Joseph's eyes grew wide. "Thank you very much, sir!" Novak echoed the sentiment.

"Happy Halloween, gentlemen."

Edison took his leave after that, leaving Joseph and Novak to hold their vigil against the dark. A whole dollar made for a generous tip—it amounted to half of their daily wage, in addition to whatever they were earning through overtime pay. Novak begrudgingly gave their boss some grace, despite the conditions. Joseph took the suggestion to pick up snacks for their all-nighter. Because of the holiday, Linwood Grove stayed open late tonight, so the younger mucker absconded with his new fortune to acquire a midnight feast, leaving Novak to guard their solitary light.

The minutes ticked by in silence. Alone for a moment, Novak reached into his chest pocket and removed a folded letter. He'd received it that morning and had carried it close to his heart all day, mulling over the words in his mind. Now with a moment of privacy, he unfolded it and read it again, hope glowing in his chest for the first time in weeks. He held the paper up to the lamplight, not fearing that he might singe the edges as with a candle.

My dearest Novak,
What wonderful news! Mirko could barely contain his excitement when he saw your second letter, and he danced all over the house when I read him the news, singing, "We're going to see Papa! We're seeing Papa!" I've told him so many stories about you that he misses you as much as I do, even though he was so young he can't truly remember when you left. He is working on a greeting gift for you now. Sweet child. I shall not spoil the surprise.

I have started preparing the farm for sale. My younger brother will be moving into the house. You remember Andrej? He is now twenty and courting a girl from the neighboring village. He shall take care of the farm and property as he is now a young man, and should his romantic interests prove fruitful, it will provide for his new family as it has provided for us all these long years. Before he can move, we must clean what we are leaving here for my brother, and sell what we cannot take with us. I will set up an auction once I have everything we want to keep organized and packed in trunks and our travel arrangements made. What we make should be enough to pay off the debts from our bad harvest year. It is quite the undertaking, but I look forward to seeing you with each passing day as I strip the house barren.

We are both intrigued by your discussion of electric lights and the promise of a magic show. Christmastide cannot come soon enough.

I miss you, but I love you, and I am proud. We will see each other again.
Sonja

Novak smiled at the page and gently turned it over. On the back, Sonja had quickly sketched a picture of Mirko dancing, a letter in his hand. The graphite smudged in places and showed that she drew it in haste, probably before she had to run the note to the postal cart to send it on time. He handled it delicately, careful not to ruin the picture any further by brushing his touch over it. Machine grease and filament fibers always clung to his skin, and his fingerprints would destroy the priceless moment captured in time by his wife's talented hands.

With the newly acquired dollar from Mr. Edison, Novak could finally afford the ticket fare for them to come to America. He would collect the money he'd stored up at home and send it first thing in the morning. Novak dreamed of the moment he could reunite with his family beneath the light of a thousand such bulbs and found himself so lost in thought that he didn't notice when Joseph reappeared behind him. He stepped out of the shadows and into the beam of the solitary light without warning, and spoke aloud.

"What's that?"

Novak spooked, wrinkling the letter in his surprise. He cursed in his native tongue, laid the letter out on the table, and smoothed down the edges, then carefully refolded it along the proper lines and slipped it back into his pocket.

"Sorry." Joseph handed him a bottle and set a basket of food down between them. Hot pretzels with mustard, funnel cakes piled with confectioners' sugar, and a paper bag full of hard candies. The rest of his change jingled in his pocket. "There was a fair in the park. I got a little distracted when I ran into some friends. Sorry I was out so long."

"I did not notice. I was reading a letter from my wife."

"Oh, I didn't know you had a family." Joseph plopped his butt in the seat and a hard candy in his mouth. "They're root beer barrels. Have you had them before? It's a new flavor!"

"They still live in the old country, but not for much longer. With any luck, they will meet me here in December." Novak cracked open his bottle of beer and took a pretzel from the pile.

"Wow! Congratulations!" Joseph raised his bottle to Novak's with a clink. "You've been here for years though, haven't you? Can't imagine that. Jenna lives far enough away as it is."

Novak rolled his eyes, but Joseph didn't notice as he'd

already swallowed his candy and started tucking into the sugary cake. To guide the conversation off his family, Novak asked Joseph about the fair, and then the Halloween traditions of the town, and Joseph talked happily to keep himself awake. As the night stretched on, they told each other tales of ghosts and monsters that might be lurking in the dark. Between the sugar and the stories, Joseph worked himself into such a jumpy state he couldn't sleep, so he took the first lonesome watch while Novak drifted off on the small cot they'd set up in the corner. After a few hours, he shook Novak awake for his turn at guard, and they traded places.

So Novak waited alone with the light. He moved to the generator and started checking over the problem parts he'd noticed earlier in the month. This had become his habit over the many, many evenings of burning the metaphorical midnight oil. Without the disturbance of the busy shop, he fell into a routine of repairing the day's mistakes. But as just one man, working on far too little sleep and far too little light, he couldn't cover every part of the machine in an evening, and there were certain parts he couldn't touch without Charles knowing he'd meddled. He worked for as long as he was able before retreating to his guard over the lamp, where he reread his wife's letter again and again to keep himself awake.

At four o'clock, in the darkest witching hours of the following morning, after thirteen-and-a-half consecutive hours of burning, the filament finally flickered out. Novak held his breath and watched it die until it left him sitting completely still in the all-engulfing darkness.

The next morning, Elias found him napping, sitting on the floor slumped against the wall. Joseph still slept on the cot, covered by a blanket Novak had brought from home, pulled up carefully over his shoulders. On the desk, a notebook lay open to a page filled with the longest string of tallies Elias had ever seen.

November 1878

Though Novak and Joseph may have told stories of monsters on Halloween night, the true monsters became the reporters who prowled the workshop day in and day out in the coming weeks. After their success with the carbonized cotton filament, Edison took their findings to the patent office, and to the press, and after that, there was no hiding from their investigations, or the roster of influential persons who all wanted a glimpse at the light. Even a judge visited one afternoon. The Wizard threw open the doors of the laboratory to seemingly anyone who wanted a tour.

NEW YORK HERALD, FRIDAY, NOVEMBER 22, 1878.—TRIPLE SHEET.

THE ELECTRIC LIGHT.

Edison Denies that His Invention Resembles Any Other.

ALL OBSTACLES OVERCOME.

Only Waiting for a Powerful Engine to Complete the Work.

"You are the eleventh reporter to-day that has made that observation" were the words, laughingly spoken by Professor Edison, in his laboratory at Menlo Park, to a HERALD reporter last evening. They were called forth by the reporter saying, as he seated himself in the chair proffered by the inventor, "I hear that the Patent Examiner in Washington has rejected your application for a patent for the electric light. How is it?"

"I don't believe it," said the inventor. "It can't be true, else I would have been notified by my Washington solicitor long before this, and I haven't heard from him to that effect. Besides," said the Professor, after a moment's pause, "my claim is so distinct from any other ever made in electric lights that the application could not on any pretext be rejected; and, again, I have applied for eight different patents to cover the invention. The rejection of one leaves seven others."

"But it is said that in 1845 a Cincinnati inventor, J. W. Starr, applied for a patent for exactly the same principle as yours."

"I am familiar with the facts of that matter," replied Mr. Edison, throwing his hat on his desk and

With construction finished on the new machine shop, the teams moved their work out back and assembled the partially finished pieces together. A score of men worked together at a time, but Novak had his hands full assembling hundreds of lightbulbs for their first private test of the generator's capabilities. Elias couldn't come into the office in the weeks leading up to the big trial: his baby had just arrived, so his family needed him at home. Charles complained bitterly about his absence and condemned his "lack of work ethic." Novak simply took on his friend's share of the work and told Elias not to return until the big day.

Eventually, the generator came together. The wiring coiled out from the hulking machine like the tentacles of a leviathan to each of the lamps stationed around the room. On a chilly Monday morning late in the month, Elias followed Novak and Joseph as they gave him a tour of their hard work and performed the last of their checks.

"Positions, everybody! Positions!" Charles called. He picked up two large cables and fitted their ends into each other with a satisfying *ckthnk*. Then he scrambled over the bundles of taped wire to the raised platform where Edison stood passively overseeing the whole affair.

"Are we ready to begin?" asked the "great inventor."

"Ready!" Charles said with a cheery, smile that didn't quite reach his eyes. "Joseph, please light the boiler."

Joseph stepped forward and lit a match. He cradled it in the palm of his hand for a moment, then inserted it into the stovepipe. After a few minutes, the water reservoirs heated enough to turn to steam and filled the room with a hissing, rattling sound. Some team members gave the huge wheels a starting spin with the help of a lever. Others adjusted the myriad of valves to control the pressure levels. The machine sputtered and whirred to life, the belts turned, and the magnetos spun, inducing current in the wired coils surrounding the chamber.

With the flip of a switch, Novak opened the relay to the lights, and they all flickered on, powered by the chugging

contraption. For a moment, everything worked as intended:
a spectacular array of shining bulbs flung their steady light to
every corner of the cavernous, crowded workshop, artificial
candles glowing brighter than the sun. The other workers gasped
and shouted in amazement and shielded their eyes. A roar of
cheering and clapping erupted from the teams. Their cries of
delight echoed off the newly laid brick walls, and for a moment,
the cacophony of cheers drowned out the din of the devil in the
device.

Then a hiss of steam escaped the boiler. Panic flashed
through Novak's mind.

"These pressure dials are way too high!" one of the
operators cried. Joseph reached for a vial with a wrench.

"Get away!" Novak screamed. "That's going to blow!"

The first operator caught his arm before he could touch
the valve and pulled him away from the stove box. The two
stumbled back from the boiler and hit the ground just in time
to escape the explosion of hot steam from the burst pipes. At
the same time, Novak shoved Elias to the floor. Shrapnel from
the metal casing shot through the air. Static electricity arced in a
flash of energy, like lightning escaping from captivity. A spray of
scalding vapor hit Joseph, who couldn't move clear in time. He
ran toward Novak and Elias, cradling his arm and face, blistered
and red. Elias caught him and helped him to the ground. *No. No!
No!*

"Help!"

"Call a doctor!"

"What do we do?"

The noise spread as the rest of the workers tried to escape
the building, and created a pileup of shoving elbows and pushing
shoulders. Smoke billowed out of the unsupervised firebox. A
tangle of twisted pipes jutted from what was left of the boiler,
like the guts of some unearthly fiend. Vicious shards impaled
whatever poor souls had stood closest. Dark blood pooled on the
bright new workshop floor. The lights flicked out without power
driving them, replaced by flames licking up the support beams.

Novak's heart dropped. All his work couldn't save their lives from this inevitable disaster.

"SHUT. THAT. THING. DOWN," he bellowed.

"Form a fire chain! Grab emergency kits! Stop panicking, and get this under control!"

His commanding voice rose above the din and brought order to the disaster. With the pressure released in the explosion, the machine sputtered to a stop, but nobody wanted to approach it again, for good reason. Eventually, Charles stepped forward from the crowd, took up a bucket of sand they kept by the door for exactly such an emergency, and threw it onto the firebox. Following his example, the men finally snapped into action. Novak ran to get cold water to treat the burn and tried to comfort the injured Joseph until the paramedics arrived to help. Edison absconded to placate the press, who'd already piled over each other on the street outside the workshop.

Eventually, once all the unconscious and injured had been carried away and only ashes smoldered in the twisted, jagged remains of the firebox, Charles and Novak met eyes across the workshop.

The fires of righteous rage lit in Novak's heart, fueled by years of condescension and petty slights, stoked by a few harsh months of sleepless nights, an overworked mind, and ignored pleas for caution. Weeks of pressure boiled over with the pain and worry of seeing innocents and friends hurt for selfish men's egos.

The boiler would not be the only thing exploding today.

Novak stormed over to Charles and seized him by the shirt, shaking him with all his might.

"I *warned* you!" he hissed. "This disaster, the lives of these men, all of their wounds, this is *your fault*!"

Charles struggled, hands clamped over Novak's, trying to worm his way out of his grip, but he couldn't pry the mucker's fingers from his pristine white collar.

"This cannot be my fault when *you* asked to perform the safety checks," Charles sneered, pointing a finger into Novak's face. "You're not good enough—"

"How *dare* you!" Novak let go of his lapel and wrenched his finger backward. Charles let out a yelp as his wrist and elbow twisted with it. "You cruel, gutless, wretched bastard! What ever happened to being the leader of the project? Take some responsibility, you wicked coward!"

Charles whimpered. Novak did not let go and leaned his face closer to the manager's. "I came to America because I wanted to make a better life for my family. I came to this workshop because Edison's stories inspired me, and I wanted to create inventions to make a better life for people all over the world. But all you do is take from the people who actually care: you take their time, you take their energy, their ideas, their health, their lives, and you trample it beneath your feet so *you* can feel accomplished without doing anything."

Now Novak released his grip and shoved Charles to the ground. He landed hard with a yelp and shuffled backward on his ass. His expression twisted with disdain. Novak gestured to the shattered remains of the generator.

"Machines can be fixed. But all these broken people? That is not so easy a task. Today, you destroyed their passion, their trust, and their loyalty. Mine most of all."

Without another word, or waiting for a response from his nemesis, Novak turned on his heel and strode out the door. Outside, fire engines and ambulances lined the streets, which were clogged with reporters and cameramen, all scrambling to get the first crack at sensationalizing a tragedy. Edison stood calmly, taking questions and dismissing them, trivializing the details to cover up the accident, and sending them away from the workshop. Novak watched for a moment, seething and debating if he should walk over and say something. In the end, he decided he'd only get in the way of the medics, and turned toward home instead.

Novak shut the door behind him, then leaned against it and slumped to the floor with a long, shuddering sigh. He rested his head on his knees and finally broke down into sobs as the fatigue, guilt, and frustration overwhelmed him in waves of heaving gasps and tears. The explosion still rang in his ears, overlaid by Charles's voice, accusing. *You're not good enough. You're not good enough. You're not good enough. You're not—*

You're not.

Not.

Good.

Enough.

Blisters. Bleeding. Pressure-blasted pipes and scalding steam. Joseph's cries. Elias's shocked expression. He had failed his men. Failed himself. Broken people. Splintered dreams.

Novak drowned in his bitterness and despair until every bone ached from sitting curled on the floor and he could wring a river from his handkerchief. Exhausted, he staggered to his bed and collapsed, still clothed. When had he last slept in this house instead of the little cot at the workshop? He couldn't remember. Eventually, he drifted off into a restless sleep.

Novak overslept through work the following morning as his exhausted body recovered from the months of grueling all-nighters. When he woke, disoriented and bleary-eyed, to midafternoon sunrays splaying across his bedroom, he found a note slid under his front door.

Dear Novak,

I meant to give you this before, but didn't get the chance. We hope you are recovering well and that you are able to make it, despite the situation.

Your friend,
Elias

Attached to the hastily scribbled note was a slightly crumpled envelope. Enclosed, Novak found an invitation in Emily's fine calligraphy, inviting him to a Thanksgiving dinner at their house, and to meet their new baby. Novak tossed the card onto his cluttered desk. He lacked the energy for a party at the moment, but Thanksgiving Day fell on Thursday, meaning he had a few days to recover before facing Elias again. Had his friend witnessed his outburst? Had he returned to work so soon?

Novak stopped that line of questioning and helped himself to a glass of water and a belated breakfast. He tried not to think about work—his mind kept returning to the explosion, his confrontation, to Joseph trembling in his arms. Though his appetite abandoned him, he choked down his plate of eggs and toast. He could tinker with a hobby project he'd left abandoned for months, but the idea of touching his tools made his hands ache. Instead, he got dressed and left, not for work, but to visit the people who actually mattered.

Joseph's eyes lit up when he saw Novak approach. Or one eye, at least. One side of his face was wrapped in gauze and bandages, along with his arm, which settled in a sling. He sat up in bed, reading, with the privacy curtain pulled back. Several of their coworkers lay in adjacent beds and smiled as Novak passed.

"Hey! I'm surprised you're here and not at the workshop," Joseph said.

Novak grunted in response. "How are you feeling?"

"Been better. The nurses are nice. They gave me something for the pain. My burns should heal alright, but there might be a lot of scars."

Novak nodded solemnly. "I'm *so* sorry. This is my fault. If I had—"

Joseph laid his free hand on Novak's. "I know how long we all worked on that stupid machine. It wasn't all on you."

"You shouldn't have been operating the pressure valves.

We knew the risk."

"And I took it willingly," Joseph said simply, "This hurts. A lot. But I can't change the choices that were made. Even if I would like to give Charles a good shakedown."

Novak couldn't help a wry smile at that. "I might have already done that on your behalf."

"Hah! Good for you!" Joseph sat up straighter, then winced and rearranged a pillow to make himself more comfortable. Novak briefly recounted their exchange to his grinning friend, then shook his head.

"Perhaps I should not have spoken so bluntly, but in the moment, it had to be said. I do not know if I can go back, as long as he remains, not after seeing what happened to you."

"You did the right thing," Joseph said. "Whether you return or not is another choice, but not one I can tell you to make."

"My family is coming. I'll need money to support them, even if it means working with a worm like Charles. You don't have that expectation. I don't think you'll be back." Novak observed.

"I don't know how long it will take me to heal. Maybe a couple months. Admittedly, it scares me to think about returning."

"And no one would blame you."

"But a lot can happen in a couple months. Who knows? I want to see the lights."

Novak sighed. The hypnotizing lights. They enchanted anyone who worked with them, or even heard of them. *What a powerful idea.* "I should check on the others. Rest. I'm glad you're alright."

Novak stood to take his leave and move to the next bed, but Joseph spoke again, surprising him. "Are you alright, Novak?" Joseph asked.

Was he? Did he even matter, when he saw the rows of hospital beds stretching down the ward? "I'm just fine, Joseph," he lied with a smile. "Get better soon."

On Thursday, he arrived at Elias's house disheveled and late after visiting another hospital and losing track of time chatting with all his colleagues. Emily opened the door with her infant in a sling at her chest and the widest, most welcoming grin on her face.

"Novak! You made it! Come in, come in, let me take your coat! Oh, Elias will be *so* pleased to see that you came."

"Thank you for inviting me," Novak said, feeling awkward at the circumstances of the invite, but appreciative nonetheless.

"Of course, of course. Have you met little Eliza? And my sister! This is Lucy..."

With that, Emily effortlessly welcomed Novak into their family's home, introduced him to their extended family, fed him, and helped him forget his worries. Not a word about work passed anyone's lips, only remarks about how big the children had grown and how delicious the food tasted. Despite himself, Novak slowly felt himself relaxing, even if he found his heart aching for his own family when he held baby Eliza. She'd come down with a bad case of colic, and both her parents and aunt grew weary of comforting the cranky child. But Novak happily rocked her the rest of the evening. Once he returned the baby to her mother, he joined the toddler and five-year-old on the floor to play with blocks. Emily once joked that if he wouldn't go back to the workshop, she would hire him as a nanny, but he couldn't find it in himself to laugh. She let the matter drop after that.

He'd forgotten how good it felt to laugh and chat with his friends outside the context of work. Despite that, curiosity lingered in the back of his mind. *What became of the project? Would Edison continue with the exhibition? Did Charles learn his lesson? Hmmph.* Novak doubted that. When it came time to take his leave, he reluctantly returned the baby to her bassinet, and Elias escorted him to the front door.

"I know you've had a rough time of it recently, but thank

you for coming tonight," Elias said, running his hand through his hair. "I'm so glad the kids like you so much."

"I am sorry I didn't let you hold Eliza all night."

"You can come by more often if you'd like, now that you have more time."

Novak sighed. "I actually wanted to ask about"—he waved his hands in the air around his head—"everything. Do you have any updates? I do not want to go back, but I cannot rest easy without knowing."

Elias nodded in understanding. "There were no casualties."

"Thank God. I've been visiting the hospitals, but I couldn't find everyone."

"It was a miracle," Elias agreed. "A few were able to get discharged straight home. Everyone survived. Mr. Edison ordered that the company pay a portion of the hospital bills, but the project is still set to continue. The press didn't get many details, only that the project had been delayed due to an unexpected failure, but that's the nature of all inventions. We'll continue, and most folks are actually pretty excited."

"That's insane." Novak scoffed.

"Charles stepped down."

"No!" Novak laughed in disbelief. "You must be joking."

"After your lecture, he reconsidered some things and called a meeting with Mr. Edison and me. While he wasn't relieved of all his duties, he recommended you to take over in his stead. I told him I would ask, but that you would only come back when you were ready."

Novak covered his face with his hand as his laughter turned to strangled half sobs. Hadn't he dreamed of this moment? Now that they gave him the opportunity to take control, did he really want to return to Edison, even if Charles wasn't his direct supervisor? Would it really make any difference in the way the shop was run? Would his leadership be able to protect any of his friends? He tried to hide his turmoil, but Elias put a hand on his shoulder and forced Novak to look into his eyes.

Elias continued, "I'm leading things in the meantime, but the men want to finish the project in your honor, and for everyone who was injured. We assessed the damage, and only the boiler suffered massive failures. But the rest of the generator looks like it can be repaired with some hard work and patience. Mr. Edison will buy a new boiler, and we'll assemble it properly this time. But they look up to you. They trust you."

The pressure of expectations and disappointment settled over his shoulders once again. Novak took a deep breath to steady himself and gave Elias a half smile. "Thank you for telling me. I will consider it."

"Nobody would blame you if you never choose to set foot in that godforsaken building again. I wouldn't judge you. Just take your time and do what you think is right, alright?"

Novak nodded and gave his friend a deep hug before returning to his house, where he spent a long time staring at the pictures around his desk. The last time he'd held Mirko, his son had been baby Eliza's age. They'd be arriving in a little over a month. He'd bought this house with an extra bedroom a few years after moving to America once he'd saved up enough for the down payment. In choosing it, he'd hoped every time he changed his calendar that this year would be *the* year his family would arrive. He kept the extra bedroom locked, empty, and waiting pristinely for Mirko to claim it. Now, finally, he could prepare the house to make it a home, like Elias's.

He couldn't buy new furnishings without a job.

He'd promised his son a magical light show.

The light show wouldn't happen unless they could fix the boiler.

Unless *he* led the team to fix the boiler.

If he led the team, he could change the work schedule, couldn't he? Instead of staying for hours after dark every day, they could all go home at normal hours if he planned properly. But what if Edison forced him to stay late? With his family in the States, he would never spend nights at work again. He should establish that rule now. If he quit and tried to work his way up the ladder at another company, he might never get the chance.

What if Charles fought him again? Novak had stood up to him once, but did he have the strength to continue that battle? He could only hope that Elias told the truth, that the coward would stay out of his way.

What if the boiler turned out to be irreparable? Or if the generator sustained other damage that Elias didn't catch? He wouldn't know unless he looked for himself. Charles's incompetence threatened to destroy the livelihoods of everyone in the shop—if Novak couldn't send money to his family, they might never make it to America.

Novak returned to work on Monday, stomach knotted with anxiety, but resolute in his decision. An enthusiastic mood greeted him when he entered the workshop. Phonographs hummed. Lights glowed. Neighbors chatted openly to ask, "Hey, mind if I borrow a screwdriver?" or to say, "How was your Thanksgiving weekend?" The shop had taken on a new life, one that Novak had never expected in the aftermath of such a traumatic event.

Elias spotted him first from his spot up on the mezzanine. "Hey! Novak's here! Welcome back!"

A chorus of *welcomes* echoed from around the laboratory, and Elias led him into the generator room, where a fresh crate sat—just delivered, still unopened—which contained the new boiler. Charles met his eyes briefly from across the room where he swept up debris. He looked at the ground and said nothing as the workers cheered for Novak. He grinned, despite himself, and clapped his hands.

"Alright, men, let's see what we've got."

December 1878

In the following weeks, Novak and the team worked diligently to mend the errors within the generator's assembly. Once given the time and support to do a full evaluation, he found several obvious problems that would have been easy catches if they had taken the effort to do the safety checks earlier. He filed all his findings into a detailed report and took it to Edison with Elias's backup, which earned them a hefty budget to complete whatever repairs they needed—no expenses spared. As long as the generator could perform in time for their exhibition at the end of the month, Edison would bankroll anything they needed. They'd delayed the event from Christmas Eve to New Year's Eve to gain another few days of prep time, but this change of plans did not dampen the shop's resolve. Elias prepared an itemized budget to order the replacement parts. Novak created a timetable that wouldn't have any man working longer than an eight-hour shift, and let people volunteer for the time slots that best suited their schedules.

Leaving at five that week left him extremely satisfied with his progress.

Every day, he checked the mail for a new letter from Sonja. He'd sent the money last month and expected a new update any day now, but he understood she would be busy with packing for their long voyage. In the meantime, he also busied himself with furnishing the house for his family. First, he finally bought a shelf for his pile of books and filled the empty spaces with magazines Sonja might like and picture books for Mirko. He threw open the locked door to the second bedroom and cleared out all the cobwebs. With the extra money from the long nights of overtime, he'd bought a child's bed set, dresser, and wallpaper to fill the room with color.

Novak also caught up on all the chores that had fallen by the wayside in the years of waiting. The house's siding desperately needed to be washed after such neglect, and mold creeped up the doorframe. After a good scrub and a fresh coat of red paint—Sonja's favorite color—the place looked completely new. The neighbors looked at him as if he were crazy, painting at dusk in the frigid December weather, but Novak's spirits couldn't be higher. Next, he trimmed back the dead, overgrown grass and cleared the sidewalk.

Inside, he decorated for Christmas, trying to copy the style of their old home as much as he could remember with the materials he could find. And gifts! He needed to find the perfect gifts to give them *in person* this year! Novak scoured several department stores until he found the perfect items: Sonja would no doubt bring some of her art supplies, but she deserved a nice workspace. He found a broken easel, fixed it, and got a fresh pack of watercolor paints and brushes to go with it. For Mirko, he came up short. *What kind of toys would a six-year-old like?*

Joseph had healed enough to be discharged from the hospital. His eye was spared from the burn, leaving his eyesight, though the other injuries still stayed covered with bandages. Novak asked his young friend to take him shopping, and together, they picked out a bright red wagon, perfect for going on adventures. Joseph also gave him a hand-me-down model train that ran on steam. He didn't want to keep it after his accident, understandably so. Novak assured him he would use it carefully. In return for the favor, Novak helped Joseph pick out an engagement ring for Jenna. He would propose on Christmas Eve, and his excitement and anxiety fueled Novak's own eagerness to welcome his family home.

With full days at the workshop as the new manager of the generator project, and full evenings of home preparations, the month passed in a blur of activity. As the date grew closer to Christmas with no word from Sonja, Novak grew more anxious and turned to watching the shipping and weather reports with a vigilance. The sea turned choppy and dangerous this time of year, and he feared one day he might receive a telegram notifying him of their deaths, if, God forbid, their liner sank beneath the merciless, frigid waters of the Atlantic.

A few days before Christmas, the long-expected letter finally arrived. Novak ripped it open immediately when he saw the heavily stamped envelope, not even bothering to go inside before he read the contents. It was dated from a week ago and scripted in his wife's hand, though messy and rushed. This time, there was no picture included. It read:

My dearest Novak,

I write to you from Dubrovnik, where I am staying in a hostel with Mirko. We had no trouble selling the farm to my brother, who is now engaged to Maria—the woman he was courting in my last letter. He now lives in our old home, and all our things are stowed away in just a few boxes and trunks for the journey. We had a very hard time saying goodbye to our families and friends, but we told them you sent your love. Mirko cried when we boarded the train to the coast. I don't think he understood what it meant to leave, until it actually came time to do the leaving. But he is very brave, and being the man of the house these last years, has comforted me much in my own grief.

I regret to say we have not found passage to America. There are few ships sailing at this time of year, fewer still making the transatlantic journey with the number and intensity of storms, none which will arrive before Christmas. If this letter even makes it to you, I am deeply sorry. We wanted to be together for the sacred feast, and your magical light show, but God did not will such a reunion. This setback does not diminish my determination to make it to you. Please do not begrudge us the delay. I do not know when I will be able to write again, for our housing is temporary and our situation tenuous. You cannot send mail back to this address. Wait patiently, and hope.

I miss you, but I love you, and I am proud. We will see each other again.

Sonja

Novak stumbled inside and slumped onto his sofa, crumpling the paper slightly in his hands as he processed the words. They were alive. Perhaps his worst fears hadn't come true, but his second-worst fears assaulted him in reality. His wife and young child stranded, vulnerable, and alone, with no way for him to come to their aid, in a foreign city. He trusted Sonja to take care of Mirko. Her cleverness and adaptability far surpassed his own, and he knew she would find her way. But his love caused him to worry for their safety all the same. His helplessness ate at his core, and knowing they were so close yet so far made the waiting completely unbearable.

Would they have to wait until spring to make the passage? In the meantime, where would they go? Back to the homestead in the countryside outside Belgrade, or could they find temporary lodging in Dubrovnik and wait for the next available ship? The lack of communication killed him. He might have helped to invent the telegraph, but unless companies bought the technology, laid the lines, established networks between major cities, maintained the infrastructure, and paid the operators, what good did his gadget do him? A couple of cables existed between Nova Scotia and Ireland, but it might be a decade before the networks reached Eastern Europe. All he could do was wait.

Novak tried to throw himself into his work to forget his woes the next day, but he found it hard to care about the project anymore. If he couldn't show the lights to Sonja and Mirko, why should he give them all his energy? The generator repairs neared completion, and Joseph had chosen the best of the tested filaments. He had a team of young muckers in an assembly line working on producing as many bulbs as they would need for both the final test and their grand exhibition. After a feverish month of productivity, they closed up shop at noon on the twenty-third. Elias looked forward to spoiling his children with gifts and enjoying the feast that Emily prepared. Joseph couldn't stand still, all wound up with nerves about his proposal to his sweetheart, Jenna. All the men buzzed home to their families to enjoy the Christmastime cheer.

Except Novak.

He returned to his house that evening and made himself a quiet, humble dinner. Too quiet. Right now, he should be traveling to New York Harbor to welcome them to America. In another world, they'd debark a ferry and meet him on a crowded dock in a flurry of hugs and kisses and shouting. They would have made their way back to Jersey, talking nonstop the whole time. Sonja's laugh should have echoed through the little kitchen. Mirko's feet should have been pattering on the stairs, exploring every nook and cranny of his new home. They should have been singing together and picking out outfits for church tomorrow.

But instead…

Too quiet.

Too still.

All Alone.

Novak flung his empty plate into the sink and retreated to the living room to read, but he couldn't stop his eyes from scanning over the page, comprehending none of the words. *Did they have dinner tonight? Were they housed under a stable roof? Was Mirko scared? Was Sonja scared, as strong as she was?*

What could he do?

The distant sound of singing pulled him from his thoughts. *O Come, O Come, Emannuel* strained through the thin windows, barely audible over the rattling radiator, but it grew louder as the source grew closer. Carolers.

Novak sat and listened for a moment as they finished at the neighbors, before realizing they would come to his house next. He needed something to do so he wouldn't just drive himself insane tonight. Before they reached his front door, he'd already grabbed his hat, scarf, coat, and gloves.

"Do you mind if I join you?" he asked as he answered their knock.

The leader, surprised but friendly, accepted his proposal and sourced a spare hymn book from among the group, so together, they set off along the route. It was only once they started walking that Novak realized Charles was among the party, and the awkwardness of his situation.

The men did not say a word to each other, as had become their custom at work. To preserve the peace of the evening, each simply pretended the other did not exist, though they were acutely conscious of the other's presence. They caroled together for several hours, working their way through the town and the hymn book, until fingers and toes grew numb, noses ran from the cold, and Novak forgot his troubles in the melodies. In the fellowship of singing with complete strangers, he'd found peace.

Eventually, members peeled off at their respective neighborhoods to return home, until only Charles, Novak, and a few other folks remained to return the materials to the church where they'd started. As they departed, the leader thanked Novak for his impulsive decision to join them, and he took his leave. But Charles followed him. At first, Novak hoped they simply needed to walk in the same direction to get to their homes, but it became clear that Charles had trailed Novak intending to catch up. Novak hurried along, eager to shake the ex-manager.

"Novak, wait!" Charles called after him.

Novak continued a couple of steps hesitantly, unsure whether to give Charles his time, then stopped and turned, bracing himself for an argument. "Yes?"

"I just wanted to say…" Charles stared at the ground. "I wanted to say good work, with everything. And I apologize. I should have listened to you before with the generator's safety. After the explosion, it's been eating me alive. You had every right to put me in my place."

Novak gaped in shock for a moment. Never in a million years did he expect an acknowledgment of his work, much less an *apology* from Charles.

"Thanks for singing tonight. I'm looking forward to the lighting test after the holiday. Merry Christmas," he said, then left before Novak could reply. Novak watched him retreat in stunned silence as a flurry of snow fell, warmth rising in his chest.

He returned home and made hot chocolate to heat his

frozen fingers before going to bed. On the day of Christmas Eve, he slept in—taking a well-deserved rest, prepared a feast for himself, then took the leftovers to a soup kitchen. After cleaning up, he prepared himself for the vigil Mass, where under the candlelight, the congregation celebrated the solemn feast of Christ's birth. Kneeling alone in his pew, he prayed for his family's safety and their voyage. That the angels would guard them as they guarded the Holy Family in their travels to Bethlehem, that a miraculous light would somehow lead his family home.

On Christmas Day, he set out his family's gifts under the tree, but they remained unopened.

Coming back to work on the twenty-sixth, the workshop buzzed with stories about dramatic family dinners and gift exchanges. Joseph beamed from ear to ear, proud to announce that his fiancée had said yes. Elias rambled about his baby's first Christmas, and how excited the older children were to introduce Eliza to all their family's traditions, despite her tiny size. Novak did not mention his own quiet heartbreak, but Charles gave him a smile and a nod when he walked in. Novak smiled back.

Today, they would test the generator again. This time, they'd taken every possible safety precaution. They took their operators from a group of volunteers and gave them special training to make sure everyone knew all the ins and outs of the machine. Each one wore protective gear and worked with a buddy who could aid them in case of an accident. Novak ordered that the most at-risk valves be fitted with pressure-release breakers to give early warning in case of a failure. Their checks had passed with flying colors.

All the same, you could cut the air of anticipation with a knife. Novak urged everyone to relax and think clearly. If anyone let their nerves get the best of them, it could lead to catastrophic mistakes, as before. He tried to project a calming presence, but internally, his stomach churned as much as the rest of theirs.

Finally, it was time.

This time, Novak lit the match and dropped it into the firebox. He refused to let anyone else assume the risk of that job if, God forbid, another explosion occurred. The heat turned the water in the reservoirs to steam. Hissing filled the room, but it remained controlled and led to a steady, rhythmic thumping. The wheels spun; the pressure stayed level. The belts turned, magnetos spun, wires buzzed to life with a frequency in the correct range and stayed there. When Joseph flicked the switch to turn on the lights, they illuminated the room with a bright, confident glow.

For a long, terrifying moment, they waited for an explosion, but none came. The generator chugged cheerfully, the bulbs gave off their light, and the steam escaped through the stovepipe out the roof of the building.

Gradually, a roar of applause, cheers, whistling, and whooping filled the room as the workshop realized the magnitude of what they'd accomplished. Elias clapped Novak on the back and dragged him into a hug. Joseph jumped up and down in uncontrollable excitement, shouting, "We did it! We did it! We did it!" Even Charles and Edison clapped for their achievement.

They basked in the glory of their lights until the fuel ran out in the firebox and the process shut down, letting the generator run out of power and the bulbs switch off, but the morale could not be dampened as they made plans to build the infrastructure for the exposition right away. Within hours, Edison filed construction permits with the city. They returned stamped and signed, and Novak's team started laying wires.

Only hours after that, the reporters descended upon them.

Edison and Charles did their best to keep them at bay, but soon, a police brigade came to set up barriers between the workers and the gathering crowd. Tourists arrived the next day. Everyone wanted a glimpse of Edison's marvelous electric lights.

NEW YORK HERALD. WEDNESDAY, DECEMBER 31, 1879.—TRIPLE SHEET.

A NIGHT WITH EDISON.

Some Flashes from a Laboratory Symposium.

MUSIC AND MATTER.

Random Shots at Many Things—The Pretenders of Science.

VIEWS OF A BOLD INQUIRER.

A Merry Scientific Supper—Carbon, Crackers and Clupea Infumata.

THE HORSESHOES STILL SHINING.

[BY TELEGRAPH TO THE HERALD.]

Menlo Park, N. J., Dec. 30, 1879.

All day long and until late this evening Menlo Park has been thronged with visitors coming from all directions to see the wonderful "electric light." Nearly every train that stopped brought delegations of sightseers until the depot was overrun and the narrow plank road leading to the laboratory became alive with people. In the laboratory the throngs practically took possession of everything in their eager curiosity to learn all about the great invention. In vain Mr. Edison sought to get away and do some work, but no sooner had he struggled from one crowd than he became the centre of another equally as inquisitive. The assistants likewise were plied with questions until they were obliged to suspend labor and give themselves over to answering questions. Not a little trouble was experienced in keeping the crowds from damaging the various apparatus in the laboratory. Requests and notices not to touch or handle were unavailing. One of the best of the vacuum pumps was broken by some over meddlesome strangers, who, during the temporary absence of the attendants, began experimenting on their own account.

MORE STREET LAMPS.

Four new street lamps were last night added making six in all which now give out the horseshoe light in the open air. Their superiority to gas is so apparent, both in steadiness and beauty of illumination, that every one is struck with admiration. The laboratory office and machine shop and the houses of Mr. Batchelor and Mrs. Jordan, were all illuminated, the total number of lights being sixty. The house of Mrs. Jordan, situated near the laboratory, has been thrown open for the accommodation of guests, and having several of the electric lamps in operation affords, perhaps, the best view of the light in actual household use.

Novak scanned the crowd for any sight of his family, but in vain. While the fame went to his friend's heads, he couldn't find any satisfaction in the attention if his loved ones weren't there to witness his work. The crowds plied them with questions, and out of politeness, they were obliged to suspend their labor to satisfy the curiosity of all. More than a few even wanted tours of the laboratory, and they had a challenge in keeping the public from touching every apparatus and accidentally damaging the delicate technology. One of the best vacuum pumps fell victim to a particularly meddlesome stranger before Novak locked the doors. The phonograph teams set up their machines outside to play music for the big event, loaded with both Christmas and popular tunes. They also kept a few, which had unwritten wax cylinders, so that passersby could record their messages or songs by whistling or humming into it and hear it played back to them. It became a nuisance to dodge the tourists, and by the day of the lighting, all the triumph of the test Novak might have felt was replaced by irritation.

Finally, New Year's Eve arrived. Novak's day was filled with frantic preparations, putting out fires, and fielding questions, but eventually, everything fell into place. As evening cloaked the city in darkness, Edison gave the command to fire up the generator. Once it spun up, Novak held his breath and flipped the switch to illuminate Menlo Park.

The lights shone against the dark winter sky. The crowd gasped and oohed and aahed at the spectacle, and for the first time, Novak felt a deep sense of satisfaction at all his work, at all the stress and dedication of the past four months. He'd helped to make all these people happy and given them a glimpse of wonder tonight.

Joseph and Jenna strolled together hand in hand, Jenna gawking at the lights, while Joseph only had eyes for his sweetheart. Elias met his family at the front of the crowd, picking up his toddler and swinging him around his head. His five-year-old danced in circles around a lamp pole, and baby Eliza had a wide-eyed stare in her mother's arms as Emily kissed her husband. Novak could only be happy for them.

Novak wandered through the crowd, admiring his work, taking in the mirth of the folks who had come for the show. Many were drinking, though midnight was still a few hours off. His friends who worked the phonographs showed him a number of silly recordings, and whenever anyone realized he was the chief engineer behind the exhibition, the surrounding mob swarmed him with questions and comments. Eventually, Novak squirmed out of the spotlight and returned to wandering, ears catching snippets of conversation as he passed groups of strangers.

"I wonder how long they can last!"

"I've heard that they can keep burning even after being submerged?"

"*Јеси ли упознао човека по имену Новак?*"

"Did you get to go inside the workshop yet? Let's go!"

Novak almost crashed into another man when his mind caught the phrase. He hadn't heard his native tongue in so long the difference almost didn't register in his ears, but he had understood the words. "*Have you met a man named Novak?*"

"*тражим свог мужа*"

Was he mistaken? Surely his ears must be fooling him. That was *Sonja's* voice. It said, "I am looking for my husband."

Novak spun around, toward the source of the familiar noise. He pushed through the crowd, searching back and forth for the face he saw every night in his dreams.

"*Помозите ми, молим вас! Знам да мора да је овде!*"

She was looking for him. She called, "Help me, please! I know he must be here."

There! To the right! He spotted a red headscarf and threadbare shawl amid the fancy hats and dresses. Red. Sonja's favorite color.

"Sonja!" he called, switching to his native language. "Sonja, it's me!"

She spun around, and her face lit up when she saw him, brighter than the electric lights, brighter than the moon or stars. Sonja, his Sonja. She ran through the throngs of people, and he ran to her, finally wrapping their arms around each other in a long-awaited embrace and spun around together. They sank into each other's warmth, pulling tightly, sobbing and laughing in disbelief and joy. She smelled like honey and vanilla, just like always. Novak never wanted to let her go again.

How! How could she be here! Could he be dreaming?

But no. A moment later, a small but mighty force caught hold of his leg and held on. When Sonja pulled away enough for Novak to see her face, she was crying and smiling and more beautiful than ever. Mirko clung to his pants, curly brown hair poking from underneath his knitted hat. Novak picked him up and swung him into the air before bringing him in for a hug too, and Mirko laughed and laughed and Novak could never imagine a more wonderful sound.

"We will see each other again"—Sonja said, echoing the closing words of every letter they'd written for the past five years—"just like we promised."

Author's Note:

In adapting a real event and real persons to a historical fiction story, some liberties must be taken with facts for the sake of the plot. In the interest of not misrepresenting real historical evidence, I want to use this space to divulge what I have changed for those who may be interested.

The characters of Novak, Elias, Joseph, Sonja, and Mirko are all entirely fictional characters of my own creation. Novak is loosely based on Nikola Tesla, being a Serbian immigrant who also studied at the University of Prague, but that is where their similarities end.

Charles Batchelor was a real close friend and associate of Thomas Edison, who worked in the shop as a draftsman and machinist, then eventually, the chief experimental assistant. In the real world, Charles established Edison's electric light company in France in 1881 and recruited Nikola Tesla to work in Edison's laboratory. Tesla would work with Edison briefly, but the two would part ways and go on to lead America in the "current wars" over AC or DC current. Because Edison is such a high-profile figure, I found it easier to typecast him into the role of the executive who is far removed from the day-to-day workings of the shop, and assign the role of antagonist to someone more personal and less well-known. But I intended no defamation of Charles's character within the story.

The timeline and technology behind the generator and lightbulb are as accurate as I can represent in fiction, outside of the boiler explosion, which I included for drama. We shall pretend Edison swept it under the rug so well it was simply excluded from the historical record. I acknowledge my friends Sahar and Greg for their advice and fact-checking on this story because, despite my scientific background, I am a chemist and not an electrical engineer. Their help is greatly appreciated.

Etta Grace is an engineer by trade and a writer by calling. She tells stories inspired by her curiosity for her science, and desire to understand the world. Her debut YA fantasy adventure novel, Runaways, features faerie folklore, magical mysteries, and strong sisterhood bonds. Etta also runs an active blog and youtube channel where she hosts book reviews, writing advice, livestreams, and interviews with indie authors. She currently lives in the Cincinnati metro area. When not writing, Etta can usually be found volunteering at her church, trying to read every book in the world, learning various hobbies from textile arts to martial arts, or spending time with her friends and family. You can follow her upcoming work on www.ettagraceauthor.com

Acknowledgments

Community is imperative in all things, and I am incredibly grateful for my community who has helped this book come to life.

To my co-authors that leapt at this project idea and trusted me with it. I am thankful for Megan Mary Moore, Jordan King, and Etta Grace who are talented writers who took an idea and helped turn it into magic.

A sincere thank you to Jordan King, who at the outset of this project commenced as an intern and partial investor, in addition to being a valued friend and co-author. His assistance and insights were instrumental to the success of this project.

To Jessica Berry, our editor. I learned a lot about editing from her and it was wonderful to see the care she took with our stories in her suggestions and feedback.

To Phil Weasley, our illustrator and book designer. Phil understood our vision and carefully and thoughtfully created pairing art that honed on both the whimsy and tension throughout our different stories. They also worked with us to set our book cover to cover. They were professional and communicative and they helped make this book of art exactly what we were hoping for.

To all of my amazing friends, thank you for always reminding me that being weird is really cool.

To the two Yodas in my life who always have room to listen and offer wisdom especially through this project. Arthur Morris: great friend, editor, and brainstormer; Aaron Davis: great friend and tech support - both talented creatives.

To my Writers Group the last two years, for their support and openness with all things writing and friendship.

To Andrea Belanger, for not only her badass photography and tech skills, but also her willingness to help me in multiple ways as I take all the new ideas I have and root for me, help me brainstorm and be an all-around amazing friend.

To Jessie Alianiello, for her continued support, friendship, and willingness to take her authentic creative voice to help me showcase this book to the world in unique and fun ways!

To Barbie Coleman, for her exuberance, business wisdom, great sense of humor and fun, listening ear and friendship.

To Noah Fischbach, who worked as an intern for me through Capital University in 2024 on other projects and in his eagerness to learn and continue helping me create and produce books, he has helped lighten the load and I have learned a lot from him.

To Evan Magill, for lending a patient ear and consistent support throughout this project.

To my mother, Nancy Green and my brother, Robert Damron for having a love of stories and always being supportive of the magical realms I choose to dive into. For being along for the ride and helping me make those a reality.

With Appreciation,

Signe Damron

Phil Weasley is a multidisciplinary creative director, illustrator, and educator whose work bridges traditional fine art and contemporary storytelling. Through Weasley Studios, they craft worlds that intertwine watercolor, ink, and digital media with themes of myth, memory, and transformation. They have taught illustration and design at the college level, guiding emerging artists in visual storytelling and creative development. Their work explores the intersections of folklore, queer identity, and creative mythmaking, inviting viewers into stories where imagination and humanity meet.

Find Phil on Instagram: @weasley.studios